I0716881

MURDER ON THE ANGELINA

A Fen Maguire Mystery

Published by Jubilee Publishing, LLC
Paperback ISBN 9781958252093

Cover design: Streetlight Graphics
Editor: Teresa Lynn, Tranquility Press

MURDER

ON THE

ANGELINA

A Fen Maguire Mystery

BRUCE
HAMMACK

Chapter One

A camo-clad figure took aim at the woman crouching behind a toppled picnic table. Showing no mercy, he pulled the trigger. A volley of projectiles struck the back of the victim's neck, driving her to the ground. Stunned and screaming, she drew back her hand covered in red goo.

From his perch on the observation deck above the melee, former sheriff Fen Maguire chuckled. The woman never saw the ambush coming.

The hapless victim rose to her feet, turned, and received another volley from a second assailant. The shots came from automatic weapons that gave a sound similar to a pneumatic wrench—short bursts of compressed air. It brought to Fen's mind the sound of a fully automatic AR-15 when equipped with a high-quality noise suppressor. He grimaced as the woman hollered for her attackers to stop shooting.

The two warriors moved on, leaving their victim to wipe paint splatters from her chest, neck, and goggles. She moved to the entrance of what looked like a Hollywood version of an urban apocalyptic setting, uttering epithets as she went. Fen looked at the smiling face of eighteen-year-old Bailey Madison by his side. If it weren't for her bandaged left hand poking out of a navy-blue sling, Fen could picture her enjoying such a competition.

"Lou got smoked," said Bailey. "Remind me not to choose her for my team if I ever enter a paintball competition."

"I don't think you'll need to worry about Lou wanting to repeat this experience. Let's get down and see if there's damage to anything but her pride."

Fen went first, taking his time to make sure he kept his right leg straight. The one thing he didn't need was to twist his trick knee. He looked up as Bailey started down the metal ladder after him. "Make sure you don't use that left hand."

She let out a huff of exasperation. "You concentrate on your gimpy knee and I'll look after my hand."

"Keep three points of contact at all times. That's good. Make sure that left wrist is hooked around the vertical bar and put your arm back in the sling when you get to the ground."

Bailey stopped her descent. "Has anyone ever told you that you sound like a bossy old woman?"

He grumbled but descended, one rung at a time. Once on the ground, he extended his hands upward, just in case Bailey slipped. She didn't, and soon stood on terra firma. "You can stop hovering over me like I'm a child." She repositioned her baseball cap and pulled the hood of her sweatshirt against the back of her neck.

Fen pulled the zipper down on his jacket to let in the cool January breeze. "This is quite a place. What do you think?"

Bailey cast her gaze to the multi-acre compound filled with all manner of paint-stained barricades. "I can see how guys full of testosterone might want to play Rambo. In fact, I wouldn't mind trying it after the skin grafts on my hand heal. It might relieve stress by pretending to shoot someone. Still, I'd have a hard time justifying the cost. I guess that's because money never came easy to me."

They walked side-by-side until finding cover in a metal pavilion where Lou Cooper sat wiping paint from goggles and the front of her sweatshirt. She looked at Fen, scowled, and kept cleaning her goggles. "If I hear one word from either of you about what a fool I made of myself, you'll both walk back to Newman County."

Bailey laughed. "Face it, Lou, those guys drilled you before you knew what happened."

The forty-something-year-old woman glared at the girl less than half her age. "Do you think you could do any better?"

Bailey tilted her head. "I couldn't do any worse. Didn't you hear them sneaking up behind you?"

"I focused on movement in front of me. Besides, the wind was whistling through the holes in this stupid plastic helmet."

Fen asked, "What did it feel like to get hit?"

Lou met his question with a glare. "I'll be glad to shoot you and let you experience it."

"No thanks. One real bullet in the knee was enough."

Lou's attempt to rub paint from her sweatshirt only smeared it. "To answer your question, it hurts. If they hit you on bare skin, it feels like a wasp sting. That guy got a couple of rounds in under my helmet on my neck. I don't know why the second guy peppered my chest when I turned around. I was already out of the game."

Fen moved her collar-length hair away and inspected the red welts. "It didn't break the skin, but they do look like bee stings. Next time, wear a thick scarf."

Lou narrowed her gaze. "There won't be a next time. I can't believe I let that crazy lawyer of yours talk me into driving all the way to College Station to do this."

Bailey slipped her injured hand out of the sling, took off a small backpack, and retrieved a sketch pad and a soft-lead pencil. "You said this was research for a story you're writing. So far it doesn't sound like much of a story."

"I doubt there'll be a Pulitzer Prize in it, but you never know what can happen when you find something novel to report on." Lou looked at the pile of stained paper towels in front of her. "One thing's for sure, there are ways to do research that don't involve being maimed. I'll stick to interviews, surfing the Internet, and searching courthouse records."

Two college-age men approached with helmets and paint-ball rifles in hand. They wore identical outfits that reminded Fen of a SWAT team. A patch on the sleeve of their camo shirts read, *Texas A&M Paintball*. The taller of the two spoke to Lou. "We came to apologize. The referee told us this was your first time. Those shots to the back of your neck must sting like nobody's business."

The second young man, distinguished by his carrot-colored hair and freckles, asked, "If you don't mind me asking, why did you want to compete against us? We take paintball seriously and compete against other universities and clubs, not newbies."

"I'm a newspaper reporter," said Lou. "I'm going to Lufkin to do a story on a professional paintball team. A supposed friend of ours thought I should get a taste of the sport before I go to East Texas."

The two young men looked at each other in a way that communicated they possessed knowledge of the team from Lufkin. The taller of the two hooked both thumbs in his tactical vest. "Ma'am. Be careful. Those guys from Lufkin play for keeps."

Lou tilted her head. "What does that mean?"

"We usually compete on closed courses. The one you were on this morning sits on a couple of acres. It's constructed to resemble a city shelled by artillery. There are lots of things to hide behind, including blind corners, dead ends, barricades, you name it.

"Things are different in Angelina County. The guys from Lufkin play unrestricted warfare on a hundred acres of thick woods. They know the terrain like the back of their hands and use booby traps, paintball grenades, mines, you name it. Some competitions last through the night."

The second young man added, "They're ruthless, and they cheat. One of them almost died last week while they were practicing." He paused. "At least that's the rumor going around." He puffed out his chest. "This much I'm sure of. They need someone to come along and take them down a notch or two."

Fen noticed Bailey sketching the two young men, but his thoughts were on the person almost killed and the accusation of cheating issued by the second student. "How do they cheat?"

Freckle-face became animated, his eyes bright. "Besides the booby traps, those guys sneak in rifles with higher-pressure air canisters than the rules allow. It gives them an unfair advantage because they can take longer shots."

The first young man spoke in a softer tone. "There are a lot of stories going around about them manipulating the natural environment to cause injuries to teams that compete on their home turf. I know for sure they bait teams into playing for money. They never lose when there's cash on the line."

The second waved his hands as he spoke. "That's not all. Last year, they competed in the Ozarks competition in Missouri and an opponent broke a leg in a pit they dug."

Fen asked, "Are you sure?" He noticed Lou had taken out her phone and was recording the students.

"Absolutely," said the redhead.

The dark-haired Aggie shrugged. "It seems something bad happens to at least one of the opposing team members whenever they have a competition."

The second student ground his molars. "Like I said, someone needs to put them in their place."

The taller of the two glanced at the phone in Lou's hand. "Are you taping this?"

"Audio only," said Lou.

A look of concern spread across his face. "If it's all the same, ma'am, we'd like to remain anonymous. We're competing against the team from Lufkin in an early-season practice tournament later this month. The rumor is those guys are planning some surprises for the other three teams."

Lou turned her phone off and slipped it into the back pocket of her jeans. "I'd like to get your names and email addresses in case I have other questions."

A look of apprehension crossed their faces.

Bailey tore off the top page from the sketch pad and handed it to the tall student. "Here's a present for you."

The two young men looked at the sketch. "Wow! This is awesome."

Bailey beamed a smile. "You look really cool in your gear."

The one with the sketch held it up for all to see. Fen gave Bailey a nod of approval. "You're shading is getting better."

Freckle-face asked, "How much do we owe you for this?"

Bailey flipped a dismissing hand, still holding her pencil. "It's not a finished product, so we'll call it an even trade if you give Lou your names and email addresses."

Lou quickly added, "Don't worry. I won't use your names or what university you attend. No one but us will ever know we talked."

The taller of the two put his hand on Bailey's shoulder. "We've been talking about a team photo." He examined the sketch again. "This is so much better. Could you sketch the entire team? We'll be glad to pay you."

Bailey gave her head a firm nod. "Take a photo of your

team. Stage it however you want, and send it to my phone. Here's my business card." She pulled a card from the back pocket of her jeans.

Freckle-face asked, "How much will this set us back?"

Bailey looked at Fen, who said, "This is your deal. Be fair but don't get greedy."

She pursed her lips together. "What do you guys think a fair price would be?"

The tall one scratched his whisker-stubbled chin. "There's ten of us on the team. The professional photographer was going to charge us a hundred bucks. Could you do it for a little less?"

She hesitated. "A hundred bucks for a complex work of ten people seems a little light."

The young man chuckled. "The price for the photographer was a hundred dollars each."

Bailey's eyelids widened. "A thousand dollars?"

Fen gave her his best stare. "Remember what I said about getting greedy? Grow your reputation and the money will follow."

Bailey huffed. "Oh, all right. Send me a photo and I'll do all ten of you for five hundred dollars."

"That's awesome," said the tall one. "If it turns out half as good as this, you can expect to get a lot more business."

Fen looked at his watch. "I hate to break up the business meeting, but we need to get going if we're having lunch with Chuck and Candy."

The two students made a special point of thanking Bailey as Fen looked on. He wondered again if the young artist would reconsider going to college or would stick to her plan of dedicating herself to becoming a professional artist under his tutelage. Once in Lou's Camry hybrid, he said, "Good job on drumming up business. What did you think of those two guys?"

"The redhead was too intense, but the tall guy seemed super nice. I bet they both have girlfriends with pretty hands."

"But can they draw and paint like you?" asked Lou.

Fen's mind went back in time to late last fall when he'd discovered the body of Bailey's drug dealer uncle floating down the Brazos River. His death left her alone and unsupervised in a run-down mobile home. After she was caught stealing some paper and drawing pencils from his booth at a local craft fair, he took a chance on helping her develop her passion for art. Returning from a craft fair, they discovered her uncle's trailer ablaze. Trying to save something of value, she severely burned her hand on the super-heated knob of the back door. Two skin graft operations later, the petite young artist was healing in more ways than one.

Bailey looked out the window but didn't respond to Lou's rhetorical question, except to say, "I'm starving."

"How does fried chicken sound?" asked Fen.

"Like I could eat an entire flock."

Fen sat in the back of Lou's Camry with his gimpy leg stretched across the seat. "Chuck and Candy may have beaten us to the restaurant. I wonder what they'll say about the paint-ballers from Lufkin."

Lou put on a blinker and spoke as she made the turn before the light changed. "I thought Candy was kidding when she told me I needed to go to Lufkin and write a story about a paintball team. This could turn into something."

Bailey took her hand out of the sling again. "Those cheaters sound like a bunch of backwoods jerks to me."

Fen didn't disagree. "Deep East Texas has some genuine characters."

"Hicks-from-the-sticks," said Bailey.

Lou pulled onto a four-lane road. "Perhaps they're just different, and that's good for a story. It's amazing how you can drive two or three hours in Texas, and it seems like you're in another world."

Fen spoke before he thought, "Deep East Texas is a land unto itself alright. I hope you're not headed into trouble."

Lou shot a quick glance in the rearview mirror. "If I survived the streets of Dallas for eighteen years, I should be able to survive in the woods of Angelina County."

Bailey spoke up. "Learn how to duck paintballs before you go."

Lou rubbed the back of her neck. "With age comes wisdom, and I've learned my lesson. No more guns of any type."

Fen kept his thoughts to himself, but something about the group from Lufkin and the serious injury to one of its members didn't sit right with him. There had to be more to the paintball team from East Texas than a bunch of cheating, self-styled commandos playing war games in the woods. Otherwise, Chuck and Candy Forsythe wouldn't be involved.

Chapter Two

Bailey wrinkled her nose. "This place looks like a dump. What did you say the name of it is?"

Fen looked around her as Lou pulled into a parking spot. "The Dixie Chicken. It's been here for what seems like forever."

"Looks like a run-down saloon," said Lou.

"That's tradition and character," countered Fen. "This place is a trip down memory lane for anyone who graduated from Texas A&M. For those old enough to drink a beer, you can bet they've bellied up to the bar inside. For the rest, they came for hamburgers, fries, fried chicken, and a game of pool."

"Whose idea was it to eat here?" asked Bailey, still sounding unconvinced about going inside the age-marred building.

"Chuck and Candy Forsythe received their undergraduate degrees from A&M. I believe they first met at this restaurant, so it's special to them."

Lou asked, "Have you eaten here before?"

He nodded. "Don't expect anything fancy. The inside

doesn't look any better than what's in front of you. It's an old-school bar with decent burgers, good fried chicken, cold beer, and pool tables. Rustic as a hundred-year-old barn."

Bailey looked across the street. "Is all that the university?"

"That's part of it. There's 5,500 acres of university property and about 73,000 students."

"Too big," said Bailey.

"You could take some art classes here," said Fen.

Bailey exited the car without responding. He was considering how to follow up when she said, "Why would I want to spend money on classes when I have you to teach me?"

Lou looked at him with raised eyebrows. "Yeah, Fen. Tell her why she should spend over a hundred-thousand dollars on a college degree."

"Who said anything about getting a degree?" He looked at Bailey, who was shaking her head. Time to attack from a different direction. "You need to realize I can only teach you some basics and what works for me. If you don't take a few classes, you'll never know what you missed. Besides, you could benefit from a well-rounded education. You could also take some business courses so you can learn how money works."

Bailey looked at the sprawling campus and then at the building that looked like the relic of a saloon. "I already know how money works. You make it and then you spend it all. Then, you make some more. It makes more sense to learn as much as I can from you, listen to podcasts, watch YouTube videos, and stay out of bars like this one."

Lou chuckled. "Out of the mouths of babes comes great wisdom."

They stepped up on what looked like the super-sized front porch of a saloon out of a Hollywood back lot and entered the building. The theme of the decor, if you could call it that, was a combination of early beer joint, weathered wood walls, neon signs, and wooden picnic tables that had more initials carved in them than any sane person would try to count. Signs, flags, posters, drawings, and carvings all paying homage to Texas A&M University decorated the walls.

A hand went toward the ceiling and waved as Fen, Lou, and Bailey walked through rows of defaced picnic tables. Chuck and Candy Forsythe were in their element, with bottles of beer in front of them.

"You made it," said Chuck. His gaze shifted to Lou and stopped. "It looks like you lost the battle."

Bailey spoke before Lou could get a word out. "She learned her lesson about going up against those guys from the A&M paintball team. She never got a shot off."

Candy tilted her head. "Why didn't you take on some beginners?"

Fen spoke as he maneuvered his bad leg under the picnic table. "We ran late this morning and Lou missed the novice group. She had to go in with advanced players or not compete until much later."

Bailey cut her eyes toward Lou. "Someone stayed up late and overslept this morning."

Lou slid in beside Bailey, facing Chuck and Candy. "It ranked as one of the top twenty most unpleasant experiences of my life. Remind me not to follow your advice again on how to research a story."

A wide smile spread across Chuck's face. "How long did you last?"

"A few minutes," said Lou.

"Minutes?" said Bailey. "More like seconds. That tall guy had you splattered and on your face before you got thirty yards onto the course."

Fen split the difference. "I'd say she lasted about a minute and a half. It wasn't a fair fight."

"Fair or not, it's the last time I'll set foot on a paintball course."

"Don't be too quick to say that," said Chuck.

Candy slid her fingers down the bottle of beer. "Your experience today will add depth to your first article in the Lufkin Daily News."

"And humor," said Bailey as she looked toward the bar. "Can we order? I'm starving."

Candy pushed up from the table. "Come with me, Bailey." She looked at Fen. "Burger or chicken?"

"Fried chicken."

"Same for me," said Lou.

A group of about fifteen university students entered and placed orders in front of Candy and Bailey. Fen quizzed Chuck. "What's really going on in East Texas?"

Chuck dragged his hand across his chin. "That's what some important people in Angelina and Nacogdoches counties want to know."

Fen looked at him. "Is this the same group that was so interested in the corruption in Newman County?"

"Same league, different team." He moved on quickly. "You probably know that the lumber industry is the lifeblood of East Texas, but the mills are having a hard time getting trees."

"Why?" asked Lou.

"That's what you're going to find out for us." The lawyer leaned forward and looked at Lou. "Let me explain. Most of the truckers that haul trees from the forests to the mills are independent drivers. When I say independent, I mean they're fiercely independent."

Fen nodded. "That usually means they don't trust law enforcement."

"Exactly. Their trucks and trailers must meet rigid safety standards in order to haul the future telephone poles, lumber, and pulpwood out of the forests and over highways on their way to mills and creosote plants. That kind of wear and tear on their equipment is a recipe for getting tickets."

Lou folded her hands. "Truckers everywhere are having a hard time. What makes these wood haulers so different?"

"Extortion," said Chuck. "In the last year, the sheriffs of Angelina and Nacogdoches counties have recorded numerous reports of vandalism and threats against the truck drivers."

"That sounds like paying protection to me," said Fen.

Chuck gave a slight nod. "You need to understand how sparsely populated this area of the state is and how dense the forests are. In Angelina County there are only about 87,000 people, and almost 35,000 of them live inside Lufkin's city limits. That means there's not much of a budget for law enforcement out in the county."

Fen added, "Extortion is hard enough to prove when people trust law enforcement and will file complaints and testify. Still, as far as crimes go, this doesn't rank in the top ten. What's the real reason you're sending Lou?"

Chuck leaned forward a little more. "The threats and acts of vandalism are turning into physical assaults. Not only that, but lumber mills aren't meeting production requirements."

Lou interjected. "I knew profit would be involved."

"Not just profit for the companies, but the livelihood and safety of the independent truckers. Two of them received broken bones last week. The story going around is they refused to pay protection to the Avengers."

Lou jerked back. "The who?"

"The Angelina Avengers. They're a paintball team."

"Yeah," said Lou. "We heard about them today at the paint-ball course."

Chuck's eyebrows rose. "Who told you about them?"

Fen took his turn. "A couple of students from the A&M

paintball team. They also mentioned a rumor about a member of the Avengers being injured."

Chuck gave his head a firm nod. "That would be Pete Crane. He's an ex-Green Beret. Someone put a paintball bomb in his mailbox. It should have gone off and splattered his chest. Unfortunately for him, he leaned over and looked in the mailbox when it went off. He lost one eye, and they're not sure about the other."

His gaze shifted to Lou. "You should know this group is as secretive as they come. Everyone is an original member, the son of a member, ex-military, or a combination of all three." He took a breath. "The sheriff has very little evidence that could lead to an arrest."

"Tell me about the evidence," said Fen.

"Footprints leading to the mailbox. They matched boots belonging to Chet Lowe, a member of the Avengers." He paused. "But there's a catch."

"There usually is," said Fen.

"Chet Lowe's wife gave him an alibi. She claims she took the boots to a thrift store a couple of days before the bomb went off."

Chuck leaned back. "This much I know for sure. Someone in Angelina County is shooting out tires as the trucks come out of the forests. They're also cutting brake lines, stealing mud flaps off trailers, and sending people to the hospital. What we need is better intel on the extent of the problem and who's doing it. That's why we're sending Lou. You'll go for a week, write a story for the Lufkin Daily News that will stir the hornets' nest, then come back to your job in Springdale."

Lou bit her bottom lip. "I'm with Fen. This doesn't sound like much of a crime spree. Can't the local reporters stir up enough stink to get some action out of law enforcement?"

Fen brought his gaze back from Candy and Bailey. "This

isn't Dallas we're talking about. Deep East Texas is a place with secrets. Sometimes they involve family members. I bet you'll find out some of the Avengers have relatives in local law enforcement."

Chuck smiled. "That's something else you can check on while you're there."

Lou let out a huff. "I thought this might lead to a book, but unless I uncover some real dirt, I'll do good to stretch this into a two-part newspaper story."

Chuck looked at Fen. "What do you think?"

He shrugged. "I'm glad I'm staying on my farm in Newman County. A fresh supply of canvases and paint arrived this week and Bailey is champing at the bit to paint. We can stay busy until late spring with no trouble. That's when we plan on hitting some festivals around the state."

Bailey and Candy returned, loaded down with plates of fried chicken and French fries. Candy bucked the trend by ordering a hamburger. She looked at Lou. "Did you get the lowdown on what's expected of you?"

"I think so. I'm to go to a sparsely populated area of the state and spend a week finding out if a bunch of survivalists are extorting money from poor truck drivers."

Candy smiled. "I expect there'll be a surprise or two for you when you dig."

"I hope so. So far, all I've received for my time is a sore neck and a ruined sweatshirt."

Fen added, "And some tasty fried chicken." He turned to Bailey. "How is it?"

She replied with a full mouth. "Mumm." She chewed, swallowed, and added, "It was a long way to travel to get chicken and French fries. Next time, leave me at home so I can paint."

Lou looked at the young woman sitting beside her. "Is painting all you ever think about?"

Bailey ran her tongue across her top teeth. "I enjoyed helping Fen solve the murder of my uncle. It would be fun if you could find another case like that."

Fen inhaled some of the breading on the chicken and fought to keep the bite in his mouth. After Bailey slapped him on the back enough times to dislodge any obstruction, he turned to her. "Enough, already. What makes you think I want to get involved in another murder case?"

Bailey held up a half-eaten chicken leg and wagged it at him. "Because you're good at two things: painting and solving crimes. I don't know how, but they fit together for you."

Candy gave Bailey an unblinking stare. "Do you sense Fen will need to go to East Texas and solve a murder?"

The question didn't seem to take Bailey by surprise. "When you're great at something, you can't help but do it. I have to draw every day. Lou writes newspaper stories because something drives her to do it. You and Chuck practice law together. Fen paints landscapes and solves crimes."

Lou asked, "But are you sensing there will be a murder in East Texas that Fen will solve?"

Bailey lifted her shoulders and let them fall. "My name isn't Claire Voyant, but I know you're a magnet for stories that reveal people with things to hide."

"And Fen?"

"He's sneaky-smart. Just when you think he's acting like an unconcerned, retired widower, he surprises you. He's always taking in what's around him, even when he doesn't look like he is."

Everyone at the table turned to look at Fen. He sat up straight. "What? I'm minding my own business eating a delicious piece of chicken. I have no intention of going to East Texas in the dead of winter with this gimpy leg."

Chuck wiped the grease off his hands. "What if there's a murder? After all, someone already put a bomb in a mailbox."

"That was a paintball bomb. Make it a real one and I'll reconsider, but only after the locals give up."

Bailey finished her prophecy by saying, "I bet the Angelina Avengers have something to do with the murder when it happens."

THE TRIP home passed without the normal chatter from Bailey. Fen believed the three pieces of chicken and the order of fries had a sedative effect on her. He nodded off himself and slept until they passed over the Brazos River and turned onto the county road leading to his property. Lou punched in the code that opened the gate and followed the gravel until it led them to the concrete driveway.

The front door opened and out stepped Thelma, Fen's housekeeper and cook. As was her custom, she wasn't smiling when Fen clambered out of the back seat with a stiff leg. She reserved her kind words for Bailey. "Are you hungry?"

"Stuffed with fried chicken. I slept all the way home." Bailey shut the car door and waved as Lou drove off.

"At least one of you has good sense. I thought Miss Lou would come in."

Fen spoke up, "She has more paint on her than one of my mid-size landscapes."

"They totally wasted her," said Bailey.

Thelma looked Fen over. "I'm surprised you didn't get in the thick of it."

"Not with this leg. I need an ice pack as it is."

With hands tented on her hips, she asked, "What did you do this time?"

Bailey spoke before he could stop her. "We climbed an observation tower to watch the paintball battle."

Fen moaned. He knew Thelma would cloud over and rain on him for climbing the tower; and since Bailey used the word 'we,' the storm would include thunder and lightning. Thelma didn't disappoint.

While the verbal tongue-lashing continued, Bailey slipped into the house like a mouse wearing socks. Thelma ended her tirade with, "Two, almost three, grown adults and not enough brains between you to fill a thimble. You're lucky they didn't have to send ambulances to pick up the pieces."

Fen tried to lessen the sting of Thelma's tirade. "Lou hated it and swears she'll never play Rambo again. As for Bailey, she thought it was silly to spend that much money pretending to shoot people."

"There's hope for both of them, but I'm not so sure about you."

The hand on Fen's shoulder came out of nowhere. He turned too fast. The next thing he knew, he was looking up at Sam, his ranch foreman and Thelma's husband.

"Drag him in, Sam," said Thelma, without a wisp of pity in her voice. "Put him in the great room and I'll bring the ice packs."

Sam grunted and bent down to place Fen's arm around his neck. This was another episode of *How-the-Knee-Turns*. Nothing new, but painful each time. As the manager lowered Fen to the couch, he said, "Road hunters killed a doe last night."

"Were you in the woods?"

Sam shook his head. "Thelma had the porch light on."

"Ah," said Fen as he considered the unusual relationship

between the Choctaw Indian and his mixed-race wife. Somehow, they always knew what the other was doing, even though Sam spent most nights living outdoors and practiced an economy of words. The burning porch light was Thelma's signal that she desired his company in the bungalow behind the garage.

Sam expanded on the report of the poacher. "Two men. Cheap boots. One shot." He reached into a pocket and withdrew the spent and mangled round from a rifle. "In a tree trunk on your side of the property line."

Fen examined it. "I'll call the new game warden and hand this over to him. Did you find any tire tracks?"

"Too dry to get a good cast. I tied a rag on the fence where they shot and another where they pulled the deer through the fence. They fired from the road on the Newman side of the property line, but the deer dropped on your side."

Fen examined the bullet again. Something about it seemed important, but he couldn't imagine why.

Chapter Three

The ring of the doorbell caused Fen's gaze to shift from the canvas. He dipped his paintbrush into a jar of smelly solvent, rubbed the bristles with a moderately clean rag, and repeated the process. Leaning back in his chair, he examined the half-finished scene of a raccoon washing its paws in a slow-moving stream. The remains of a juvenile perch lay beside the woodland creature that looked like the cartoon character of a bank robber.

He preferred to paint scenes that didn't include the harshness of life in the woods, but this was a commission requested by a client who had a thing for raccoons. They'd even provided a photo of the furry angler, caught enjoying a late breakfast.

The knock on the door to his studio brought Fen away from the great outdoors and he hollered, "Come in, Thelma."

A creak reminded Fen he needed to oil the top hinge of the door that separated his workspace from the rest of the world. "Mr. Fen," said Thelma. "This is the new game warden, Dwayne Roebuck."

Fen's hand shot up and he gave an exaggerated wave for

both to enter. "Come in, Dwayne. I've been meaning to call you and welcome you to Newman County." He pointed at a chair covered with a paint-stained drop cloth. "Take that off the chair and have a seat." He shifted his attention to Thelma as soon as she came into his field of vision. "Is there coffee?"

"If I'm in the house, there's coffee." She cast her gaze to the young man who looked as if he could benefit from three good meals a day for several weeks. "You're not married, are you?"

He shook his head.

"I can tell. You need some meat on those skinny bones. Gals around here like something to hold on to."

A pleasant shade of red, something between pink and cranberry, rose up his neck to a large Adam's apple. Past that it merged with skin reddened by the sting of winter's wind.

Fen gave his cook and housekeeper a brief scowl and said, "Coffee, please."

Thelma turned. "Coffee for two and a slab of apple pie with a wedge of sharp cheddar cheese for Officer Dwayne. You'll have to wait until after supper for yours. You need to do something about those love handles."

The door clicked shut as Dwayne sat on the edge of the chair.

"Please excuse Thelma. She's used to speaking her mind."

The young game warden smiled. "That's alright. I've been called worse than skinny. A piece of homemade apple pie will be a treat."

Fen sat on his stool. "What can I do for you?"

"This isn't strictly a social call, even though I've heard a lot about you."

"This sounds serious," said Fen. "Mr. Newman must have called you. Was it before or after I left a message with you?"

"Who told you?"

Fen chuckled. "No one. How long have you been on duty in the county?"

"Four days." He held up three fingers. "Make that three days on duty and one day moving."

"A little more time and I wouldn't have to explain," said Fen, under his breath, but loud enough to carry.

"Explain what?"

"It's a long, sad story, but I'll give you the condensed version. Mr. Newman is my former father-in-law. My wife had a weak heart. She underwent a transplant, and we thought all would go back to normal. Over time, her body rejected the new heart. Sally believed someone else deserved a second heart more than she did. I honored her wishes and didn't pressure her to change her mind. Now Mr. Newman blames me for her death. His property is next to mine, and he's a bitter old man who thinks money can fix anything."

Silence filled the room for several seconds. It seemed as if the young game warden didn't know what to do with the information, so Fen helped him out. "The question running through your mind is, 'What does an old grudge have to do with someone road hunting?'"

Dwayne nodded. "He claims someone who lives on your property shot a deer late last night."

Fen shifted in his chair. "There was a deer killed after midnight, but the shot came from the road and it wasn't from anyone on this property."

"How many people live here?"

"Four. Myself, Thelma, who you've met, Sam her husband, who's also my ranch and farm manager, and Bailey Madison. She's a recent addition who lives in her own apartment above the garage. She's eighteen and we're both artists. It's a long story of how she came to live here."

Fen reached in the pocket of his jeans and took out the

remains of a spent round wrapped in a napkin and handed it to Dwayne. "This killed the deer. I doubt if there's enough left to do you any good, but I can tell you where the shot came from, which tree Sam dug the slug out of, where the deer dropped, and where they pulled the doe through the barbed wire. No tire tracks."

He pointed. "Go back to the road, head toward the main highway, and look on your right for two strips of cloth tied to the fence about forty yards apart. The first one is where the shooters dragged the deer through the fence and onto the road. That's my property. You'll find hair in the barbed wire and blood on the gravel. The second strip of cloth is on Mr. Newman's fence. That's where the poacher took the shot."

"Who discovered the crime scene?"

"Sam."

"When?"

"This morning."

"Why didn't he call it in?"

"He doesn't like cops."

"But you were the sheriff."

Fen nodded. "It's complicated. A long time ago, they wrongfully convicted him of killing someone. I put together the evidence that got him out of prison. That makes me the exception to Sam's rule about not talking to law enforcement unless he has to."

"I'll still need to get a statement from him."

"Anything you get will come out of the mouth of his attorney, and it will be a repeat of what I told you."

Dwayne rubbed his chin. "Was Sam in the woods last night?"

"He was in the bungalow behind the garage with his wife."

Fen could tell the new game warden was running out of questions and took pity on him. "If you want my opinion on who killed the deer, look for someone who doesn't live in this county."

"What makes you say that?"

"Mr. Newman has the money and determination to find out who's road hunting near his property. I have Sam, who normally lives outside, day and night. Everyone who owns a rifle in this county knows not to mess with Newman or Maguire property, livestock, or wildlife. A few have tried and regretted it."

Dwayne leaned forward. "Where would you recommend I look?"

"Check with fellow game wardens in the surrounding counties. Collect names until you get a list of poachers with a similar M.O. Road hunters are sneaky, but not bright. The deer you're looking for is a four-year-old doe with plenty of fat."

"How do you know that's the deer that was shot?"

"Like I told you, Sam lives outside almost all the time. He knows every deer, squirrel, and rabbit that lives on this property."

The door opened after Thelma gave a knock with her foot. "You two quit talking about that deer. Ain't nothing gonna' bring her back."

Fen's phone rang. The name SAM came up on the caller ID. The call might have lasted twelve seconds before the device rested on the table beside Fen's chair.

"That was Sam. He heard a shot from the road that runs between here and the bridge. It could be your poacher back for second helpings."

"How far down the road?" asked Dwayne as he sprang to his feet.

"Close to last night's shot, but definitely past our property line. That puts it on Mr. Newman's land. Expect dispatch to call you."

Thelma clucked out a series of tsks. "They'll be sorry for shooting Mr. Newman's deer."

Dwayne quick-walked across the room, speaking as his long legs covered the distance in no time. "Thanks, Sheriff Maguire."

Even though it had been over a year since Fen wore the sheriff's badge, he had an urge to hop in his truck and help the game warden chase down the poacher. Thelma noticed his body language and shook her head. "You look like an old coon dog who's chained to the porch while the young dogs are hot on a trail."

He didn't deny it, but didn't want to give Thelma the satisfaction of reading him so accurately. "There's no use that piece of pie going to waste. I've worked up an appetite painting this afternoon."

Thelma held on to the plate. "You said waste, as in w-a-s-t-e. It's your w-a-i-s-t that you need to work on. You're too young to have that belly slopping over your belt."

"I'm the same weight now as in college."

Thelma headed for the door with the plate of pie in hand. "You might weigh the same, but parts are gettin' rearranged. It's all because you won't do what the doctors say and get that knee fixed."

"I don't want plastic and metal parts in me."

"Suit yourself, but don't expect me to feed your sweet tooth until you can work off some of that weight you've been gaining."

The door shut behind Thelma, leaving Fen to sulk and wonder if his cook would follow through with her threat to cut off desserts if he didn't agree to have knee replacement surgery. On the one hand, it was extortion and bribery combined. On the other, Thelma was a good woman, pushing him to do what would be best for him in the long run. He realized it would only be a matter of time before he succumbed to the need for relief from the pain, but not yet. It would be in his timing, not Thelma's or anyone else's.

The ringing of his phone took away all thoughts of pie and cheese. Fen thought it might be Dwayne Roebuck giving him a report about the apprehension of a poacher. Instead, the caller ID displayed Chuck Forsythe's name and number.

"Hey, Chuck. Are you still in College Station?"

"Yeah. Candy and I just walked out of a meeting with a group of people interested in what's going on in East Texas. Another man landed in the hospital in Lufkin with multiple broken bones in his right hand."

"Another truck driver?"

"Yeah. It'll be weeks, or months, before he can shift gears. I called Lou and told her to leave right away."

"Do you want me to go with her?"

"Not yet, but call her daily and get updates. If you sense she's in danger, we'll switch to Plan B."

"I didn't know there was a Plan B."

"You're Plan B."

"I was afraid you'd say that."

Chuck surprised him with his next question. "Have you met the new game warden?"

"He stopped by a little while ago. We had a road hunter kill a deer last night. Mr. Newman tried to pin it on either me or Sam, but that's expected."

"There's not much quit in Mr. Newman, is there?"

"No quit and no lack of hatred, either."

"I don't have much time to talk," said Chuck. "Get with Dwayne Roebuck and pump him for information. He grew up in Nacogdoches and knows that neck of the woods well. He should be an excellent source of information about what's going on along the Angelina River. Between him and the information you and Lou glean, we may get a good idea of how serious a problem we're facing."

Fen wanted to slap his forehead. He'd done a poor job of finding out the new game warden's background. Seemingly unimportant bits of information had a way of fitting together to give complete pictures of crimes and how to solve them. It made him realize how rusty he'd become in listening.

He wondered again if the relatively minor crimes in East Texas warranted the time and talent of a prize-winning newspaper reporter and gave voice to his concern. "Can't the locals handle this?"

"That's what I asked the group. I believe it's a bunch of local rednecks with one or two leaders who need some jail time. Candy thinks there's more to it and so do most of the others."

Fen chuckled. "If Candy thinks so, you better listen. She's a lot smarter than me and you put together."

"That's why we're sending Lou for a week. We're also brainstorming ways to send you in if things continue to escalate."

Fen looked at the half-finished painting on the easel in front of him. The raccoon needed more mischief on his face. Was he trying to say something about the events in Angelina County? Perhaps.

"Is Candy worried about Lou going into the dark woods of East Texas?"

Chuck hesitated before he said, "She'll rest easier when Lou comes back to Newman County." He paused. "If you have any ideas of how we could send you without raising suspicion, let me know."

"Nothing's jumping into my mind, but I'll think about it."

The call ended with the standard salutations, which left Fen staring at the raccoon. "Mischief," he whispered.

Chapter Four

"Summarize your week for me," said Fen as he shifted his phone from his left ear to his right.

Lou expelled a full breath that sounded like an accumulation of disappointments. "It's been a waste of time and money. Six nights in a hotel and eating in restaurants that all get their supplies from the same source. No wonder there's so much heart disease in East Texas."

"Keep talking. You must have learned something about the Angelina Avengers and their trouble with the truck drivers."

"Nothing I couldn't have learned by doing research from the comfort of my couch. All but one victim lives outside Angelina County. If the Avengers are behind the beatings and damage to trucks and trailers, they cover their tracks well."

"That fits with what Dwayne Roebuck told me."

"Who?"

"The new game warden. He grew up in Nacogdoches and describes the Avengers as local heroes in Angelina County, and a pain in the neck to everyone else."

"I can confirm that," said Lou. "They're viewed as something like Robin Hood and his merry men, except they wear camo instead of tights. They might extort money from some locals, but they also spread it around to the needy in the county. They reserve most of the serious violence for those who live in the neighboring counties or locals who refuse to pay. There's hero worship because they always win their paintball matches. The local paper runs articles singing their praises for showing the county to be the home of winners."

"Were you able to discover the leader of the pack?"

"The team's captain is a guy named Leroy Clover, but he's not the alpha male. He may have been at one time, but he no longer competes. It's more or less an honorary title."

"Did you speak with him?"

"We met this afternoon. He stuck to what sounded like a script written for him. Of course, he denied any involvement in criminal activity and kept going back to the team's winning record. I still don't know who's the leader of the pack."

"People love a champion," said Fen before he took a sip of hot tea. He lowered the mug and asked, "Is there much interest among law enforcement in putting an end to the assaults or damage to equipment?"

"That's as big a joke as me coming here to do a story. These people, especially those that live outside the city limits of Lufkin, are what I call socially inbred." She paused. "That's harsh, but you get the idea. Everyone knows everyone and their family histories. They don't trust anyone they consider outsiders, and there's a long list of unwritten rules about outward politeness but divulging nothing of value. I could live in this county until I died, and they'd still call me a move-in."

"What will it take to get someone to talk?"

"Be a third or fourth generation worker born and raised in this county with no ties to the press."

He considered the answer, which further confirmed what

he'd learned from Dwayne. Nacogdoches County was different because it boasted a city with a good-size university. Professors, students from all over, and enough graduates who fell in love with the historic town and remained, all called Nacogdoches home.

Except for the occasional turnover of the top brass at the lumber mills and a few other companies, the residents of Angelina County lived their lives and died within a thirty-mile radius of where they were born.

Another loose end occurred to Fen. "What did you find out about the guy injured by the mailbox bomb?"

"Pete Crane. He's a local who went to college in Nacog-doches, where he was in the ROTC program and went into the service as a second lieutenant. He moved back to Lufkin after he left the service as a captain. According to his military record, he was the real deal with a squeaky-clean record."

"That's a shame. He trains for war, comes back home and almost gets his head blown off." Fen heaved a sign. "Did you get enough to write a story?"

"Barely. Candy made arrangements with the editors of the newspapers in the adjoining counties to publish the story. It went out today."

"What about the newspaper in Lufkin?"

"The owner of the LUFKIN DAILY NEWS told me he wouldn't publish it unless I did a total rewrite. He only wants stories that show Angelina County in a positive light." Lou let out a sigh. "I can't say I blame him. After all, there's precious little hard evidence that the Avengers are anything but a very successful paintball team, and he has to live here."

"How did you slant the story?"

"Heavy on circumstantial evidence. I even stooped to use the cliché about where there's smoke, look for fire."

"Make sure you don't get burned."

"I'm not staying long. This is a hit-and-run job, like those paintballers from A&M attacking me."

Fen couldn't help but laugh. "Newsprint ink versus balls of paint shot from stubby rifles. Who will emerge victorious?"

"I don't really care as long as I don't have to do a follow-up story. It would take something drastic to get me to come back."

Fen wondered if this was idle chatter or a prophecy. "Are you leaving in the morning?"

"I checked out of my hotel and spent the day following up on dead-end leads. Only one left. There's a Mexican restaurant that hasn't put me in the hospital yet, so I'll stop for supper, talk to someone who says they have information, and drive home tonight."

"It's the dark of the moon," said Fen. "If I remember right, those tall trees make it seem like you're driving in a tunnel. It's a different world at night, so keep your eyes open." He wished Lou a good night and a safe trip back to Newman County.

Out of instinct, he reached for a sketch pad and pencil once he placed his phone on the table. He abandoned everything about style, composition, and formal training. The pencil flowed on its own. Strokes came fast. The shading appeared with quick wipes of a rag. Time lost its meaning until he put down his pencils and a blackened cloth. He stared at the night scene of headlights shining on a black ribbon of highway. Arms of trees along both sides of the road intertwined above to form a canopy of blackness. The perspective was from the driver's seat of a car with headlights punching holes in the pitch black with minimal illumination to the bar ditches on each side. In the rearview mirror shone two headlights, close and menacing. They looked like the eyes of a stalking predator. He shivered, closed the cover on the sketch pad, and went to bed, taking his phone with him.

Sleep came in bits and pieces until sunrise brought Fen from under the covers. The morning passed as usual, with Sam giving a cryptic report that nothing eventful occurred on the farm during the night except for a couple of feral hogs who'd wallowed out a mud hole near a spring in the southernmost corner of the property. He promised there would be no shortage of bacon and ham if they didn't move on.

As for Thelma, she rattled on about current events in town and around the county as she cooked a poached egg and grits for Fen's breakfast. The clock read 8:05 a.m. when he asked, "Bailey's not up yet?"

Thelma wiped her hands on her apron. "What kind of question is that? You know she stays up way past midnight. If she's not paintin', she's on that computer or her phone doing Face Chat or whatever they call it these days." She turned to face the stove. "Don't see why people won't pick up the phone and talk to each other. These days you don't know if the tweets and squeaks coming back at you are from real people or some machine halfway around the world."

Fen knew better than to respond. Thelma woke each morning looking for a debate, and she didn't care which side she defended. Tomorrow she might sing the praises of Artificial Intelligence and how it will make workers more productive. To defend against being trapped, he kept the mug of coffee close to his lips. If Thelma wanted to ramble or pick a fight, he'd take a drink, or pretend to do so. If she had a legitimate question, he could lower the mug and respond.

"Is Miss Lou coming home today?"

Fen lowered his mug. "She should have made it home late last night."

Thelma shook her head. "She wasn't home thirty minutes ago. I checked with Mary Ruth."

"Perhaps she put her car in the garage or Mary Ruth slept through Lou's arrival."

"Not Mary Ruth," said Thelma with absolute certainty. "After Tommy Ray died, that woman turned into a human motion detector. It doesn't matter if it has two legs or four, she can tell you what moves at night around her home. I pity the burglar who's dumb enough to set foot on her front porch after ten at night. Tommy Ray left her a twelve gauge with shells loaded with rock salt. All that new sheriff has to do is look for someone with a sore backside."

Bailey chose that moment to enter the kitchen and plop down in a chair across from Fen. Her hair was a nest of tangles while remnants of toothpaste spittle clung to the left corner of her mouth. Fen handed her a paper napkin and motioned for her to dab away the residue.

He was too late. Thelma appeared with a wet paper towel. "Child, you need to splash that pretty face with cold water the first thing every morning. Nothing like January water to put pep in your step."

A shiver started at the top of Bailey's head and worked its way into her shoulders. She then spoke through an uncovered yawn. "I don't do cold water in winter."

"How 'bout a mug of hot chocolate with marshmallows?"

Bailey nodded. "That's the perfect way to wake up when there's frost on the ground."

Fen looked at the young woman's left hand. "You forgot to wear your sling."

She shook her head. "I didn't forget. It's itching and keeping it in the sling makes it worse. Besides, the doctor said it would help the healing if blood flows down into it for part of the day. I have to be careful and not grab anything though." She then looked out the window and sighed.

Fen put down the bi-weekly newspaper and focused on the young woman. "You're not your usual bubbly self this morning. What's bothering you?"

She shrugged. "I don't know." She turned to look at Thelma. "Before you get the thermometer or reach for castor oil, it's not physical."

"Then what is it?"

"Bored, I guess. I finished the drawing for the paintball team from A&M and they paid me the full amount. I haven't heard from anyone else." She released a sigh of disappointment.

Thelma moved to the table and stood looking down at Bailey. "I told my mama I was bored and regretted it for the next three months. She wrote out a list of chores that kept me hopping from the first crow of the rooster until the last dish went in the cupboard."

Fen looked at Bailey in time to see her eyes roll upward. He had to admit, the city girl from Houston was a fish out of water on the rural landscape of a large, isolated farm in Central Texas. She needed interaction with people her own age, but she was determined not to return to high school. She wanted to get her GED instead. Also, she'd expressed no interest in college. Earning as much money as possible in the shortest time occupied most of her waking thoughts.

Thelma delivered Fen's breakfast as silence took over the room. A flash of inspiration came to him. At least he hoped it was inspiration and not one of his foolish ideas. "Bailey, you have your choice of going back to high school or taking the GED test. I want an answer today."

She straightened her spine. "I've already made up my mind about that. I'll take the GED test."

Fen gave a nod of approval. "That's fine. You have the

study guides. I'll call the school counselor and see when they offer the next test. I want that off your plate as soon as possible. You and I are hitting the road and you're going to earn enough to buy that truck you've been drooling over. To do that, you'll need a large back stock of paintings to sell that will supplement what you make selling caricatures."

"I didn't realize there were festivals in the spring."

"They start in the spring and go through Christmas. Now is the slowest time of year, so use the time wisely."

A light of excitement came into Bailey's eyes. She issued her first smile of the day and said, "I thought you were going to tell me I had to take college art classes if I wouldn't go back to high school."

"I'm not giving up on you taking some college classes, but the timing needs to be right. Come to the studio after you finish your breakfast and we'll map out the spring and summer craft fairs and festivals."

Bailey looked at Thelma. "Can I have bacon, three eggs over medium, and toast?"

"Do you want grits with that?"

"Grits are nasty."

Fen scowled at Thelma. "All I get for breakfast is a bowl of grits and one poached egg."

This brought no response or apology from Thelma.

His gaze shifted to Bailey. "From now until you pass your GED, you'll study three hours every morning. After lunch, you can paint as much or as little as you like." He added, "Bring your laptop once you finish breakfast. We'll make a list of places to go this spring and possibly summer."

Bailey quizzed him on towns and festivals until Thelma delivered her breakfast. Between bites, she was full of questions about the festivals and the potential profit from each. The harvest festival they worked the previous fall served as a blueprint for how they'd set up their displays, but she had some ideas to make it better. Fen had to confess Bailey's excitement had a contagious effect on him... until his phone rang.

"Chuck," said Fen after he swiped his phone to life and punched the green button.

Without a salutation, Chuck began, "Details are sketchy. Lou's in the hospital in Nacogdoches. They found her wandering down a logging road this morning wearing nothing but panties and a bra. It was down in the high forties last night and the initial reports are she's suffering from mild hypothermia."

Fen scowled. "I spoke with her last night. She was following up with a lead, having supper at a Mexican restaurant, and driving home."

"They found her car in Angelina County, but she was deep in the woods on the north side of the Angelina River. That places her in Nacogdoches County. It's all I know."

Fen pulled his hand down his face. "Get me the exact location of where they found her car and where they found her. I'll take Sam with me. We'll know a lot more after he examines the two locations."

Fen rose as Bailey said, "I want to go with you."

He shook his head. "Not this time."

"You'll need me to drive her car home."

"Sam can do it. Lou can ride with me. Your job is to study and paint."

Bailey huffed, "I'll agree this time, but when this turns into an actual case, I'm going to help you like I did last time."

Fen had his phone in hand. "Sam, get to the house as soon as you can and bring what you need to track in the woods of East Texas."

Chapter Five

Fen's phone vibrated and rang at the same time. He'd just crossed over the Brazos River bridge on his way to Springdale, the county seat of Newman County. Somewhat put out by the interruption to his pondering of Lou's kidnapping, he looked at the caller ID and pushed the icon that showed Candy Forsythe's name.

"Stop by the office," said Candy. "I have clothes for you to take to Lou. It seems they didn't steal anything but what she had on. Her suitcase, handbag, license, credit cards, and cash are in her car."

He huffed in disgust. "Probably kept what she had on as souvenirs. I wonder if they have a clubhouse with photos of their victims and articles of clothing tacked to the walls."

Instead of responding to his comment, Candy simply said, "It sounds like you're already on your way. Is Sam with you?"

"Yeah. Unless you have a better idea, we're going to the site of the abduction first and then to where they picked her up."

"You'll have hours to think about how you want to proceed with the case. They towed and impounded Lou's car after discovering it abandoned this morning. I'll send you the GPS coordinates of where they found her and her car."

"Let's hope the deputies didn't tromp all over the crime scenes."

Sam let out a grunt of agreement.

"Anything else from your sources?"

"Nothing yet. Chuck has phone calls in to several important people. I'll keep you posted."

"What about Lou's physical condition?"

"There's nothing wrong with her voice. Her language could use a little cleaning up, but if I'd been left mostly naked in the middle of a forest on a chilly night, I'd probably use words that could take the paint off the walls, too."

"That sounds positive. Better to have her spitting fire than sulking in the fetal position."

Candy chuckled. "I'm not sure Lou Cooper's ever been in the fetal position."

Fen ended the conversation by saying, "After a night of having to walk to keep from freezing, followed by a full day of interviews with doctors and detectives, she'll probably sleep all the way home."

"Don't count on it. She impresses me as a woman who can run a long time on anger."

Sam gave another grunt of agreement, but didn't waste words.

"I'll swing by your office," said Fen. "I hope you packed warm clothes for her."

"Plenty of layers. See you in a few minutes."

The stop proved brief, as Candy had no updates to offer. In mere minutes, Fen had his quad-cab truck outside the city limits, heading east. He knew with Sam along it would be a quiet trip which would give him plenty of time to calm his jangled nerves and place bits of information into various mental folders. It took an hour of driving before he abandoned irrational thoughts of revenge. Once he cleared his mind, he turned to his tried-and-true method: pretending he was high above a make-believe table with notecards containing individual facts waiting to be placed in logical order. It was a strategy that served him well as sheriff. Powerful emotions hindered judgment. Still, occasional thoughts of firing a TASER into the faceless body of the person who'd orchestrated Lou's abduction came to mind.

He glanced to his right and considered the solid, stoic person in the passenger's seat. Sam was a man of few words, but when he spoke, each word served a purpose. It didn't surprise him when Sam's chin rested on his chest and his breathing slowed to that of a state of sleep.

They crossed I-45 at Centerville, the appropriately named town that split the distance between Houston and Dallas. The modest hamlet was a good place for a bathroom stop, to fill up with gasoline, and buy snacks. Not only was the town halfway between the two largest population centers in the state, but it also served as the unofficial boundary between Central and East Texas.

Before long, they passed through the town of Crockett and the Davy Crockett National Forest. A text from Candy gave him the map coordinates he needed. A second text arrived that read,

Lou's car found about two miles north of the Angelina Rifle and Pistol Club. DPS Lieutenant to meet you at the shooting club.

He pulled over and drew a circle on an old-school road map that marked the location of the gun club. "Lou said she was following up on a lead on her way out of town. I bet she stopped by the Rifle and Pistol Club to meet someone."

Sam nodded and said, "Could be. Or she stopped somewhere else, the kidnappers took her from that location, and put her car near the shooting club to give us a false trail."

Fen pulled his hand down the side of his face. "You check the parking lot when we get there. Look for signs of a struggle, or anything else that seems odd. After we're finished, we can go to where they found her car."

The miles clicked by on eastbound Highway 7. Tall pines in Davy Crockett National Forest swayed in a cool easterly breeze, as if they were dancing to slow music. Sam kept his gaze focused on the towering, dense forest. "This is how land should look."

They traveled out of the national forest, but the scenery didn't change much, except for modest homes and a few businesses that looked as if they hung on to life with dingy fingernails. After turning off the main highway, they drove down a farm-to-market road until they turned onto a county road. They soon arrived at the near-empty parking lot of the gun club. Fen stated the obvious. "Not much going on today."

Both men spilled from the truck and Sam began a head-down walk that took him to the edge of thick woods.

Fen considered what story he'd devise to legitimize his presence. He also considered the questions he wanted to ask about Lou's abduction. Perhaps the Highway Patrol Lieutenant could tell him more about the Angelina Avengers. His gaze shifted from the outdoor pavilion covered with a tin roof to the parking lot's entrance. A blue Mazda four-wheel-drive pickup, decked out with large knobby tires, turned off the county road and headed straight for him.

The driver parked on the passenger's side of his truck. A

woman stepped out sporting a purple baseball cap with SFA embroidered in bold, white letters. She appeared to be in her mid-thirties, but the jacket and the scarf around her neck made it difficult to tell. With a nod of her head, she asked, "Fen Maguire?"

He tried not to act surprised, but his cracking voice gave him away. "Uh... yes. I'm Fen Maguire."

She took confident steps toward him. "I'm Lieutenant Angie Morse." She showed him her badge. "You probably don't remember me, but I met you once when you were a state trooper. I believe it was shortly before you had to retire."

"That was a long time ago. You have an excellent memory."

"There aren't many troopers who get shot in the line of duty then go on to become a county sheriff. It also helps that you're a celebrity because of your paintings." She laughed. "I admire artists, but I can barely print my name where anyone can read it, let alone paint a landscape."

While she talked, Fen took a better look at the lieutenant. What arrested his attention was the wide, green eyes set in an oval face. His look must have turned into a stare. She tilted her head and asked, "Did I smear mustard on my face again?"

He blocked her question with an upraised hand. "I'm sorry. It's a horrible habit I picked up from sketching caricatures. In that discipline, you look for a prominent physical feature, the one that enhances the subject's beauty or personality the most, and you exaggerate it. I was double tasking by listening to you and imagining how I'd sketch you."

The corners of her full lips rose. "You must mean my bug-eyes. That's what my brothers used to call me. You should see them when I'm surprised." She parted her eyelids wide to give him a sample.

Fen shook his head. "Their symmetry and color are amazing. I've never painted that exact green before. It would take some experimenting to get it right. Eyes are difficult; that's why I usually stick with nature scenes."

She looked away after a slight pink showed in her neck.

"I'm sorry," said Fen. "I didn't come here to talk about painting. It's obvious someone contacted you and told you to meet me here."

She straightened her posture, nodded, and asked, "Where's Sam?"

"Do you know him, too?"

"Of course not. Candy gave me his name. She wasn't sure where you'd go first, but I had a hunch you'd stop here before you went to where the deputy located Lou's car."

He cast his gaze toward the thick trees surrounding the parking lot. "Sam's out there somewhere. He's not fond of crowds, strangers, and especially anyone that wears a badge and gun."

"Candy warned me not to expect much interaction. Can't say that I blame him. Being falsely charged, convicted, and imprisoned makes people distrustful."

It was time to move on. "How far to where they found Lou's car?"

"Two miles by road. One as the crow flies."

"I'll follow you."

Angie scanned the wood line. "What about Sam?"

"He's already there or on his way."

"In that case, ride with me. It'll give me a chance to fill you in on what I know, even though there's not much."

The doors slammed shut in close succession. Angie began her narrative as soon as the seatbelt clicked. "The information I'm going to give you is from sources in the Angelina and Nacogdoches County sheriff's departments. Some of it comes from the officers' reports, some from Lou's statement, and a little more from other sources. Do you also want rumors and speculation?"

"Give me everything. I'll separate the wheat from the chaff later."

She spoke again after clearing the parking lot and turning onto a red dirt road. The blacktop ended at the gun club's entrance. "According to Lou's statement, she believes a lone assailant abducted her shortly after dark last night." She threw a thumb over her shoulder. "It took place in that parking lot. Only one man spoke and it was in short, clipped sentences with an exaggerated hillbilly accent."

"Let me guess," said Fen. "She parked near the trees on the right side. He came out of the woods on her blind side and had her door open before she saw anything."

"That's correct. He pepper-sprayed her and had a hood over her head before she saw anything. After forcing her out of her car, he secured her hands and ankles with zip ties and put her face down in the back seat of her car. If there were two abductors, she never heard, saw, or smelled the second. We believe they drove the road we're on now until they turned onto a trail through the woods. A couple of hundred yards down the abandoned logging road, the driver transferred her to a cargo van. With her eyes burning from the pepper spray, and trussed up like a Christmas turkey, she lay on the floorboard of the van for about thirty minutes."

She paused and shifted her gaze to him. "That might not be accurate, because the pepper spray pretty well disabled her. But the distance to where they found her in Nacogdoches County works out pretty well with the timeline."

Angie had to slow for a sharp curve, downshifted, and sped up as she came out of the corner.

"Once they arrived, the perp cut the zip ties on her ankles and took her deep into the woods."

"How many minutes did they walk?" asked Fen.

"Lou guessed he quick-walked her for about ten to fifteen minutes before stopping. He told her to face a tree. He cut the zip ties, but the hood stayed on. That's when he told her to take off everything but her bra and panties. Instead of assaulting her like she feared, he had her hug a tree and count to a hundred as loud as she could. She counted to twenty and tried to take off the hood. He stopped her by putting what felt like the barrel of a weapon to her back. After a firm reprimand, the voice told her to start over. She heard no footsteps leaving as she shouted the countdown again. This time she made it to sixty-seven before she jerked the hood off." She paused. "The only thing he left her was a bottle of water."

"Interesting," said Fen. "He knew she'd use it to flush her eyes. It seems he went to great lengths to capture her and not do any permanent damage."

Fen stopped speculating and asked a direct question. "What about smells in the van? Or any sounds she might have heard on the way or in the woods? Did she mention anything unusual?"

"You'll need to follow up with her on that. There was nothing in the report."

"When did they recover her car?"

"That's a bit of a story within a story. After they found her in Nacogdoches County and determined her identity, they notified Angelina County. The responding deputy claims he wasn't told it was an abduction. That may or may not be true. He said he believed the car belonged to a college student, out camping on private property. He tagged it and moved on. That caused a delay in responding and impounding it."

Fen narrowed his eyebrows as he looked straight ahead and spoke to himself as much as to Angie. "Didn't know? Didn't care? Miscommunication? Or was it a sympathetic deputy helping teach Lou a lesson?"

Angie shrugged. "That might be why they sent for you."

He wanted to explore the attitude of law enforcement regarding the Angelina Avengers, but she slowed the truck and turned down a path with fresh tire marks. It was nothing more than a relatively straight path through tall trees and a couple of ruts where trucks had traversed in the past. After driving about a hundred yards, Sam emerged from behind a tree with hands up like stop signs.

Introductions that Sam didn't respond to came and went. Angie shot Fen a knowing glance and stood back.

"What did you find?" asked Fen.

Sam motioned with his finger crooked for them to follow him. He walked about thirty yards further, spoke as he went, and pointed at the ground. "Tow truck." He moved on. "Tracks of van or pickup." After another few steps, he pointed at indentations in the sandy soil. "Police SUV, and Lou's car tracks."

He turned and explained. "The van came first, followed by the car. Scuffle. Lou fell down here and one person drug her to the van. The car stays while the van leaves. Police stop here. The cop goes to driver's window, goes back to his car and leaves."

Fen nods. "We understand he tagged the car for towing."

Sam grunted agreement with Fen's statement. "Tow truck comes and takes the car."

"Have you had time to search the woods?" asks Fen.

"The man that drove the van walked from here to the parking lot of the gun club. Too dry to get a good cast of his footprints. I haven't looked around here yet."

While Sam searched the surrounding woods without snapping twigs, Fen turned to Angie. "What's your gut tell you about Lou's abduction?"

She took off her baseball cap and held it in her hands. "If Lou wasn't a big-time newspaper reporter, I'd say it's a college prank. There used to be a lot of that stuff go on, but that was three or four generations ago. I think someone took offense to her article and replicated something done at SFA in the sixties or seventies."

Fen mouthed the letters and said, "Stephen F. Austin State University. I didn't have the Angelina Avengers pictured as college guys."

"A couple are students, and some of their parents might have taken some classes. No graduates besides Pete Crane, the victim of the mail box bombing. It's a straight shot from Lufkin to Nacogdoches up Highway 59. Only about thirty miles."

"What else can you tell me about the Avengers?"

"They're multi-generational expert hunters, fishermen, and woodsmen. Their skills transfer well to paintball, which has been around for quite a while. Several are ex-military. They take it seriously. Many people wear camo hunting in the piney woods of East Texas, but these guys wear it all the time."

"What about the stories of extortion and thefts?"

"They're true, and the M.O. is like what happened to Lou in some ways, but completely different in others. They hit fast, faces covered, minimal talk, and exaggerated hick accents. No one's getting rich off what they're doing, but they're like mosquitoes when you're camping. Drive you nuts."

Sam came back and announced, "Nothing in the woods. Everything that happened last night took place on this road and in the parking lot."

Angie turned and walked back to her truck. Once she covered the relatively short distance, she said, "You two hop in." She stopped and looked around. "Where did Sam go?"

"Back to my truck. Like I said, he's not very sociable." Fen spoke over the hood. "Do I follow you to where they discovered Lou this morning?"

"After I drop you off at the gun club, you're on your own. You won't have any trouble finding your way with GPS coordinates and Sam." She opened her door. "I'll give you a business card. My private cell number is on the back. Use that to call me, but only if you get in trouble or we need to talk. This is your show and I'll keep a low profile."

They both climbed in and Fen asked, "Has anyone ever asked you to do something and you weren't sure it was worth your time?"

Angie delayed starting her truck. "The Avengers haven't done anything real bad yet, except plant that bomb in a mailbox. We believe they did that because of some sort of internal power struggle." She put the truck in gear but didn't release the clutch. "I'm not saying they don't need to be stopped. Their crimes have gotten worse for over a year—bolder, hurting more and more people financially. This may not be a murder case like your last one, but there's no telling what these guys are capable of."

Fen nodded. "Point taken." He didn't say anything but wondered if Angie was stretching the seriousness of the abduction and the mailbox paintball bomb. The phrase 'fraternity prank' rattled around in his mind like a rock in a metal bucket. Was Lou's abduction some sort of rite of initiation?

Best not bring up that possibility to Lou when he picked her up from the hospital.

Chapter Six

Between the GPS coordinates supplied by Candy and Sam's keen eyes, Fen had no trouble finding the spot where a hunter found Lou walking down a logging road. Before slipping his phone back into the pocket of his jacket, he checked the messages. He'd missed one from Lou that read,

Get me out of this hospital. NOW!

He realized it was already mid-afternoon but he and Sam hadn't tracked Lou's trek through the forest. This left him in a dilemma. Should he stay with Sam and help look for evidence, or go to Nacogdoches and retrieve Lou?

Sam was a step ahead of him. "This is where they found her. I'll meet you back here after you get Lou." With that simple statement, Fen knew Sam would follow her path into the woods, find out where her abductor dropped her off, and return to this exact spot.

By the time Fen turned the truck around, Sam had completed his search of the immediate area and was entering the woods. It would be foolish to ask if the Choctaw tracker needed water or a snack to take with him.

Once the tires on Fen's truck were once again on blacktop, the maps program on his phone charted the course for him to follow to the hospital in Nacogdoches. The drive gave him time to ponder how to proceed with an investigation, or if it was even worth his time to do so. After all, he was no longer officially in law enforcement, only a used-to-be cop with a private investigator's license. Yet, important people in the shadows believed something serious was going on in Angelina and the surrounding counties. From his perspective, nothing had happened yet that couldn't be handled by the local sheriffs' departments. He wished he'd questioned Angie more thoroughly about corruption, or other reasons the local police hadn't done more to corral the paintballers.

Traffic thickened as he came into one of the oldest cities in Texas. It wasn't long before he pulled into the parking lot of the hospital and strode into the main entrance. A smiling volunteer greeted him and directed him down a maze of hallways to the emergency room. A not-so-smiling nurse took the bag of clothes from him and told him to wait while she retrieved Lou. Her terse instructions came with commentary. "I'm glad it's you riding home with that potty mouth and not me. I've seen a lot of mad women in my day, but this one wins the blue ribbon."

"I thought she might have calmed down by now."

The nurse sputtered a laugh and spoke over her shoulder. "You'll need earplugs."

Fen made his first mistake by asking Lou if she needed to do anything to check out of the hospital. Her eyebrows came together. If looks could kill, he'd be on cold, stainless steel in a morgue.

She spoke through gritted teeth. "Since I seem to have misplaced my purse with my insurance card and my credit card, I need to find someone who can tell me how to get out of this God-forsaken place." Lou took a deep breath. "Please tell me you stopped in Lufkin and picked up my purse so I can avoid a stack of paperwork."

"Uh... I thought it best if Sam and I started the investigation first. If you need..."

She gave him a look that could turn steam into snow. "Don't even think about being chivalrous and paying for this."

Lou turned and stormed down the hall, muttering, "This is just perfect." She continued toward the front of the building and didn't stop until she looked down at the smiling volunteer.

"Good afternoon. How may I help you?"

Lou's tone was tight as undersized shoes. "I need to check out."

The woman asked Lou's name and lowered her gaze to a computer screen as she typed. "Oh dear. Someone should have come to you and worked out a plan for payment before you left the ER. You'll need to talk to someone about financial aid before you can leave."

Lou leaned over the counter and whispered, "Look on your screen again. Does it show my name, address, and phone number?"

"Well, yes, but you can't leave until—"

That's all the woman got out before Lou spun on a heel and headed for the door with Fen walking in her wake.

The passenger's door to the truck slammed shut. Lou looked out her window and said, "No questions. Take me to my car."

Fen made the second mistake of the day. "One stop first. Sam's in the woods where they found you this morning. We need to pick him up on our way to Lufkin."

She threw up her hands and raised her voice. "Why not?

I'd like nothing more than to revisit the place of the greatest embarrassment of my life."

He swallowed. "You're right. Let's go on to Lufkin to get your car. Sam is more at home in the woods than we are sitting in our living rooms."

She spoke through clenched teeth. "Stop patronizing me. Go get Sam. I need to hear first-hand what he knows about the Huckleberry who kidnapped me."

Silence reigned as Fen retraced the route to the logging road. Sam stood from the log he'd been sitting on after the truck came to a stop. He piled in the back seat and waited to speak until prompted by Lou. "What did you discover?"

"They dropped you off, took you on a walk to disorient you, and left. I found the place they had you hug the tree. It was only a hundred yards into the woods. You turned the wrong way in the night and walked away from the main road."

Fen thought about asking if Sam found any physical evidence like a cigarette butt or a candy wrapper but, given Lou's state of mind, he didn't chance it. If Sam had found anything, he'd say so when the time was right.

Lou wasn't judicious with her words. "Wonderful. No evidence, no suspect I can identify, nothing but a huge medical bill. Can this day get any worse?"

He cringed. That's one question Fen learned never to ask. He took out his phone and called Angie Morse.

"I didn't expect to hear from you so soon. Did you retrieve Lou?"

He gave an affirmative answer and asked, "Where's the impound yard?"

"What time is it?"

Fen looked at the display on the dashboard. "Six-fifteen."

"How far are you from Lufkin?"

"I can be there in twenty minutes."

Angie let out a sigh. "The local wrecker services have their own impound yards and the one they took Lou's car to closed at six. She won't be able to get it until tomorrow."

Fen could feel Lou's gaze burning into the side of his head. "What about her purse?"

"It's at the sheriff's office. I'll call and tell them you're on the way."

He gave her a positive response and thanked her. A turn of his head revealed two squinting brown eyes and cheeks rosy with rage.

"I heard," snapped Lou. "Take me to the sheriff's office and then to a hotel."

The third mistake Fen made was telling Lou she should ride back to Newman County with him.

In a mocking tone, she responded. "What a wonderful idea. That will leave me hours away from my car with no way to get back to this God-forsaken thicket of trees and hicks. How clever of you, Sheriff Maguire." She took a breath. "Like I said. The only place I want you to take me is to get my purse and then to a hotel."

Silence took its turn for most of the trip until Lou jerked her head around and faced him. "Who was that you called?"

"A Department of Public Safety lieutenant named Angie Morse. She was waiting for us at the gun club where the person abducted you. She then took me to the spot where they abandoned your car and put you in a cargo van."

The reporter's curiosity in Lou must have overshadowed her anger, as she said tersely, "Details. Don't leave anything out."

Fen relayed the day's events from the time he and Sam arrived at the gun club until he arrived at her hospital room. He could almost see Lou writing notes in her mind that would go into a future story.

"What's Lieutenant Morse's opinion of my kidnapping?"

Fen made his fourth mistake of the day by not being more diplomatic in his response. "She said it sounded like a repeat of a fraternity prank from a few decades ago."

Sam groaned as soon as the words reached him.

Lou took in a full breath. "That's the icing on the cake. Even the state police are minimizing what happened. I expected it from the good-old-boys who roam these woods, but not from a female DPS lieutenant." She sat silent for a few seconds and lowered her voice. "Mark my words. I'll have my day with these people. They've picked on the wrong reporter and they're going to learn a lesson about the power of the press. I won't be back in Newman County for another day or two. I have a firsthand account of what it's like to be kidnapped to write. That will make a great headline in Lufkin's newspaper."

"Be careful," said Fen.

Lou scoffed. "Chuck and Candy expect me to stir things up around here. Tell them I found a very large spoon."

Not wanting to make mistake number five, Fen didn't offer to go with Lou into the sheriff's department. He also didn't ask what kept her inside for a good thirty minutes. Instead of using words, Lou simply pointed until they arrived at a hotel.

Pretending to leave, he pulled forward and found a place to park. Sam piled out and watched from behind a pillar outside the hotel's entrance. It didn't take long before he was back in the truck. "She paid. We can go home."

It seemed they might be leaving Lou in harm's way, but Fen dismissed the thought as silly musing. There was no telling how many harrowing situations the reporter had put herself in while chasing stories in Dallas. The chances of harm coming to her in a well-maintained, brightly lit, newer hotel were next to zero.

Sam seemed to read his mind. "Quit worrying. Nothing

will happen to her until she writes something else that makes people mad."

That was enough for Fen to abandon any urge to stay. "You're right. Do you want to stop somewhere for supper?"

Sam pointed to the road leading out of town. "You'll need gas by the time we get to Centerville. The filling station has hot dogs, jerky, and those little doughnuts covered in powdered sugar. Thelma won't buy them because the sugar makes a mess."

Fen hoped the convenience store/service station had something more substantial than hot dogs, but he'd make do with whatever they found to tame the beast growling in his stomach.

As the lights of Lufkin disappeared into the night, he tried to open a conversation with Sam. "I'm surprised you didn't find something in the woods where they left Lou."

"I did." Sam reached into a leather pouch he always carried and the whisper of paper being unfolded reached Fen. A reading light shone down on a stained clipping from a newspaper. He took a quick glance before the light went off.

"Is that the article Lou wrote?"

Sam grunted a positive response.

"Was the stain I saw on it from paint?"

"From a paintball that's in my other pocket." said Sam with certainty.

"Where did you find it?"

"Under the tree he made Lou hug. He poked a hole in it."

Fen could see the scene in his mind's eye. "They left the clipping there for her or the police to find and wanted her to know they didn't appreciate her story."

Sam remained silent. His job was to find and report, not to theorize about motives or intentions.

"Did you find any tracks that might be usable?"

"They walked through one muddy spot close to the tree.

There's a good footprint there if the cops don't walk by it again."

Fen took out his phone and told it to call Lieutenant Morse. She answered through a yawn. "You caught me reading in bed."

"Check the weather forecast before you go to sleep. The deputies missed a good footprint close to the tree Lou hugged. If it rains, we'll lose a solid piece of evidence. Also, Sam found a newspaper clipping along with a paintball. Someone did a lousy job gathering evidence."

Angie sounded more awake with her response. "I'll get a cast made of that print tonight if I have to do it myself."

Fen added, "Tomorrow morning, I'll deliver the newspaper clipping to Chuck. He's good at fixing awkward situations."

The phone went back into the pocket of Fen's vest. He said nothing else until they approached Centerville. Sam might have been asleep, but was more likely admiring the land with so few people, homes, and lights. The quiet gave Fen time to ponder the day and Lou's reaction to it. He had little doubt her anger would abate until she published something that would build on the first article. The Angelina Avengers would feel the sting of her words.

He tapped his fingers on the steering wheel. Would the paintballers lie low for a while or continue their mini crime spree? He wondered if he should devise a plan to spend time in Lufkin or Nacogdoches to gather more information.

The lights of Centerville seemed especially bright after coming out of the dark woods. He pulled up to a gas pump and Sam was out the door and gone before he could unscrew the gas cap. The stop might have lasted ten minutes.

Back on the road, it seemed odd there were so many lights, even in the remote areas. His thoughts went back to East Texas and the value of returning to do a thorough investigation. He'd need a cover story that would give him a reason for staying in either Nacogdoches or Lufkin. A memory of his trip to College Station jarred loose in his brain. The members of the Aggie paintball team said there was a tournament somewhere along the Angelina River. It would take place not long after the spring semester started. "Lou won't miss that," he mumbled to himself and thought he'd better take steps to make sure she wasn't left hugging any more trees in her unmentionables.

His thoughts turned to Bailey and what to do with her if he spent an extended stay in East Texas. Oh well, he'd cross that bridge later. One thing at a time. Lufkin or Nacogdoches? What cover story could he come up with?

By the time they reached home, Fen had the outline of a plan. It would need massaging, fine tuning, and some help from people with influence, but he could envision himself painting a landscape on the banks of the Angelina when he wasn't gathering information that would lead to arrests.

Chapter Seven

Sleep evaded Fen after 4:30 a.m. Yesterday's rushed trip to East Texas and the flood of sensory input had his thoughts flying in several directions at the same time. He needed to corral them and knew exactly how to do it. It would require a carafe of coffee and at least forty-five minutes in his office.

Thelma had the coffee maker set on a timer, so by the time he showered and shaved, hot stimulant was waiting for him. By mutual agreement, she wouldn't appear for another hour. Armed with a steaming cup, Fen strolled to his office, closed the door behind him, and took the urn holding his late wife's ashes from a bookshelf. He placed it on a table directly in front of him. Coffee and talking to Sally was how they'd started their day ever since they exchanged wedding vows. They'd always told each other their plans for the day. Her transplanted heart stopped beating over a year ago, but the ritual continued. It wasn't what the grief therapist recommended, but it worked for him, and he saw no reason to change the routine simply because the communication was now decidedly one-sided.

At ten minutes to seven he placed the urn back in its place

of honor, the bookcase between two photos, one of him and Sally together, and one of her alone—eager for life, alive, and so beautiful it defied words. He whispered the same thing he told her every day of her life with him. "You're the only girl for me. Always will be." He followed this part of the ritual by relating his plan out loud, but in a whisper-soft voice. If he closed his eyes, he could see her nodding in agreement or wrinkling her brow at something that needed more thought. He never paid attention to time, but the sessions rarely went over thirty minutes. Today it went into overtime.

Halfway to the kitchen, the phone in his pocket jangled a series of notes, and he looked at the caller ID. "Good morning, Chuck. You're up early."

"No earlier than any other day. How was your trip?"

"Noisy after I picked up Lou. She couldn't get her car out of impound until today, so she stayed the night."

"I heard. It sounds like it also wasn't the finest day for either sheriff's department. I understand you have some evidence to give me."

Fen continued his trek toward the kitchen. "Sam used gloves to pick it up, so it's possible there's DNA on it. Also, I came up with a plan to get me to Nacogdoches, but I'll need help."

"Come to the office as soon as you can."

He could tell by the tone of Chuck's words that the mere mention of a plan pleased him. Having one wouldn't ensure success, but it always helped. Most of the time, his plans worked, but not always.

Fen wanted to keep things light, so he asked. "Will Candy make the coffee? I don't know what she does to make it taste so good."

"She'll have your favorite mug waiting for you. Can you come early? I'm booked solid from eight-thirty on."

"I'll grab a piece of toast and be out the door." He pushed the disconnect icon and shoved the phone back into the pocket of his vest.

Thelma had the kitchen door open, so it came as no surprise that she'd dipped into his conversation. With hands tented on her hips, she fired her first salvo of the day. "You aren't going anywhere until you've had a proper breakfast, not service station junk food like you and Sam ate last night. There's a glass of juice on the table. Start with that. You've already had three cups of coffee and you're going to have one or two more at that lawyer's office." She huffed as she put a skillet on the stove to heat. "As hopped up as you get on caffeine, I don't know what keeps you from swingin' from the rafters."

He knew better than to speak the pithy comeback trying to fight through his closed lips. Instead, he took a drink of orange juice. Thelma's monologue continued as she lay three strips of bacon in the skillet. "You'd better have a good reason for leaving Lou in that town with someone who gets their jollies from kidnapping women, stripping them down to nothing more than a bathing suit would cover, and leaving them hugging a tree. What kind of man would do that to a woman?"

"Good question."

It was obvious Thelma had extracted every detail of the trip from Sam.

She rattled on about how she'll feel better when Lou returns to Newman County, away from the crazy world where people shoot each other with plastic balls filled with paint and played war games in the woods. The longer she talked, the more Fen tuned her out and focused on the question that went straight to the heart, her question about what motivated the man to risk abducting Lou.

Why would someone go to so much trouble to embarrass her? The simple answer was revenge for the article she wrote criticizing the Avengers. Most of the time, the simple answer was the right one... but not always. He'd file the question of motive away until he had more facts and evidence. He hoped some would come from Chuck and Candy.

The rattle of a plate coming down in front of him brought Fen out of a semi-trance. He thanked Thelma and hurried through his meal. On the way past his office, he remembered the paint-stained newspaper clipping inside a plastic sandwich bag. His next stop was Springdale, the hub of Newman County, the location of the county courthouse and Chuck Forsythe's law office.

Candy unlocked the door, allowed him to enter, and locked it behind him. He preferred early morning coffee with Chuck and Candy rather than trying to squeeze in five minutes between Chuck's clients and incessant phone calls.

Chuck looked across his desk and got right to the point. "Tell me your plan."

Candy presented him with a cup of coffee and Fen began. "Lou's provided us with basic background information, stirred things up, and now has a grudge to settle with the Angelina Avengers."

Chuck interrupted, "She called Candy last night and said she'll stay in Lufkin until the follow-up story is ready to print. It could be several more days. I spoke with Lieutenant Morse. She's keeping tabs on Lou as best she can, but she can't be expected to give her around-the-clock protection."

Fen nodded his approval. "If they wanted to harm Lou, they would have done it two nights ago."

He took a sip and continued, "There are three things I want to accomplish and two of them involve Bailey. First, I need a cover story to get back to East Texas and I have to make it look like I belong there. If I could get an invitation from the university to come as a guest lecturer or instructor in the art department, I wouldn't arouse suspicion."

Chuck looked at Candy, whose smile reached her eyes. "Brilliant. The spring semester will start soon, so I'll make phone calls this morning. What are the other things you want to accomplish?"

"Bailey is intent on earning money so she can buy a truck. We made plans to work at a variety of fairs and town celebrations this spring. That's her priority. Mine is, I want her to experience college, so she doesn't have any regrets later in life. Right now, she's dead set against it. The only way I see that happening is to ask her to enroll in college classes in an undercover capacity to help me with this investigation. I understand some members of the Avengers are students at the university. Neither me nor Lou stand a chance of getting close to college students, at least not like a pretty young lady could."

Chuck asked, "What about Bailey wanting to work fairs and earn money?"

"She and I can still do that on weekends." Fen added, "There's one more thing that could derail this plan. Bailey doesn't have a GED."

Candy spoke up. "Wasn't she set to graduate from high school this spring?"

He nodded.

"How were her grades?"

"She made A's and B's without cracking a book."

"I'll take care of it," said Candy. "Expect her diploma to arrive in the mail by the end of the week."

Fen rested his mug on his thigh. "That was easy."

Chuck's eyebrows pinched together. "I'm concerned about the wrong people finding out you and Bailey are working together. You unloading her luggage at a dorm might raise eyebrows."

"I considered that," said Fen. "We'll need to travel separately and lead separate lives. She'll be a college student from Houston and I'll be a visiting art teacher from Newman County."

Candy asked, "Do you think she'll go along with it?"

"She won't at first, but she'll warm up to it after we negotiate and she gets what she wants."

Candy stood. "You make a much better father than I thought you would."

Fen shook his head. "Don't hang that title on me. When it comes to dealing with Bailey, I'm a widower making things up as I go. Wish me luck in talking her into going to college. I'll need it."

FEN CONSIDERED MAKING a few stops on the way home but realized everything about his plan needed to come together for it to work. By the time he entered the kitchen, Bailey was awake and finishing her breakfast. She looked up from a bowl of cereal. "Where did you go so early in the morning?"

"Come to my studio when you're finished and I'll tell you."

"Uh-oh," said Thelma. "Watch out when Mr. Fen wants to have private meetings. It means he's up to something. Sometimes it's good, and other times he's spinning a web that you might get caught in."

Fen looked at Bailey, who cast a suspicious gaze his way. He kept a straight face, turned, and walked away.

Thelma let out a huff. "It's a web for sure, Bailey, and you're the fly. Watch him close, honey. He can be sneaky as a politician up for reelection."

Fen loaded three colors of paint onto his palette and added details to the front paws of the raccoon. It wasn't long before

Bailey joined him, settled in a chair, and watched as he added minute nails to tiny paws. She studied the strokes and said, "I'd have left it as it was."

"Every brush stroke I'm adding at this point is worth another fifty dollars to the sale. If it was fifteen years ago, I would have left them off, too. Patience and practice increase the price."

"Is that a lead-in to what you really want to talk about?"

He quirked a hit-and-run smile. "How would you like to help me with an investigation?"

Her eyes brightened, then faded. "That's a loaded question. You know I'd love it, but something tells me there's a pile of pooh that comes with the pony."

"There always is. It all depends on how much you want the pony."

She settled back into the chair. "What's the deal?"

Fen continued to paint as he explained. "I'm going to Nacogdoches to investigate some people involved in extortion, aggravated assault, and kidnapping."

"You're talking about that paintball team." It wasn't a question the way she said it. "Thelma filled me in at breakfast. She told me what you and Sam did yesterday. She also said you left Lou there."

He cut his gaze toward her and then reloaded his brush. "I'm glad she told you. That means I won't have to waste words on how this is serious and has the potential to get even worse." He took a breath. "Some members of the Avengers are students at SFA in Nacogdoches. It's being arranged for me to be a guest instructor for the spring semester."

She crossed her arms. "Are you telling me you're going back on our agreement to work shows this spring?"

"Absolutely not, but we'll need to concentrate on weekend fairs in East Texas. Nothing west of I-45."

Bailey remained silent for a long second before she said, "Your plan to include me doesn't make sense."

Fen liked to use silence at this stage of negotiations. Bailey was nibbling on the bait but wasn't ready to take the cork under. He squirted small amounts of paint on his palette and mixed them with a clean brush. Pleased with the color, he applied sure strokes to the river in the painting.

"That's better," said Bailey.

"Raccoons are unusual animals. They like to dip their food in water when they eat, which causes small circles to radiate away from them."

Bailey expelled a huff through her nose. "I have so much to learn."

Fen used her confession to move on. "That brings us to what I want you to do for me."

"Here comes the pooh," said Bailey, with suspicion lacing her words.

He moved on before she could say anything else. "You don't have to worry about studying for a GED. Don't ask how, but you're getting a high school diploma this week."

Her eyes opened wide. "How awesome is that?" She stayed silent, but not for long. "Hold on. The diploma is another pony, which means more—"

Fen didn't allow her to finish her sentence. "It means I need someone young and smart to get to know the Avengers who go to SFA."

It didn't take Bailey long to put the pieces together. "You won't let this college thing go. Still manipulating me to do something I don't want to do."

"It's only for the spring semester. You choose the courses you want to take."

"How many?"

"You'll need to take five to be a full-time student."

"Can they all be art classes?"

"Only two."

She grumbled under her breath. "What about me building up the number of paintings to sell? I'll need to paint, not go to stupid classes."

"You'll have plenty of free time and you can use the university studio."

"Where will we live?

"You'll live in a dormitory."

"That's more pooh." She shook her head. "It won't work."

"Why not?"

"Do I look or act like someone that would fit in with girls living in a dorm? Besides, I have to rely on you for transportation. All it would take is for one Avenger to see us together, do a Google search on you, and they'd know you were a sheriff and I was up to something."

Bailey wrinkled her nose. "Besides, you know I'm a loner. I can't think of anything worse than living around a bunch of spoiled, rich girls."

Fen didn't cut her any slack. "That's the price you pay for doing undercover work. We don't always get to choose our companions."

She immediately came back with, "What's the pay?"

"Free room, board, classes, and the chance to make a lot of money at fairs this spring."

She shook her head. "You're losing me. You'll need to up the ante."

He put down his brush and gave her his full attention. "You're right about one thing. To make this work, we can't let anyone know that you're investigating the Avengers or that you know me. My cover is that I'm a visiting instructor. You'll be a freshman student whose focus is art classes."

He waited for a response that didn't come. "It occurs to me you'll need something to drive."

She rolled her eyes. "I have six hundred dollars. That will buy me a bicycle, but nothing with four wheels."

"I was thinking of something more like a used truck with a camper shell."

"Did you hear how much money I have?"

"I heard. You told me to up the ante, so that's what I'm doing. Find a good used truck and we'll deck it out with a camper shell like mine, with racks for paintings."

She scooted to the edge of her chair. "Are you saying you'll buy me a truck like yours?"

He nodded. "Something similar, unless you want a minivan or an SUV. I'll take care of the insurance, gas, maintenance, and repairs until we work some fairs."

Bailey rose and extended her good hand. "Mr. Maguire, you have a deal. I'll be a college student for one semester and do my best to get to know members of the Angelina Avengers in return for one awesome used SUV. It will be more convincing than if I show up in a soccer-mom's hand-me-down."

"Let's not make it too awesome. I retain the right to approve or disapprove your choice."

They shook hands. "Deal."

Bailey left with a spring in her step and Fen had a wave of satisfaction roll over him he hadn't experienced in a long time. The good feeling was short-lived when he realized he might be placing Bailey in danger.

Chapter Eight

Lou's Camry eased to a stop as Fen slid the last painting into the custom rack in the back of his pickup truck. He waved and continued packing for his trip to Nacogdoches.

The slamming of the car door preceded Lou's examination of his cargo. "You've been busy."

He nodded. "Completing works I began a long time ago. I got in a habit of starting, but not finishing, landscapes after Sally died. It didn't take too much to get them ready to sell."

Lou looked longingly at the rows of canvases. "I'll have you paint something for me when I become a famous author."

"What would you like?"

"Something without pine trees."

He chuckled. "I thought you were a tree-hugger."

Her eyelids narrowed. "Not funny. Tell me about Bailey. When did she leave?"

"Yesterday morning. Thelma loaded her down with enough food to last half the semester."

"Did they both cry?"

He put a folded easel in an empty spot, speaking loud

enough to be heard outside the camper shell. "Not Bailey. She pretended college was no big deal, but the hug she gave Thelma said something different."

He backed away from the bed of the truck, then glanced toward the house. "Speaking of Thelma, don't go near the kitchen if you know what's good for you. If you look up separation anxiety in a psychology textbook, you'll see Thelma's photo."

Lou proved she was nobody's fool. "I'll steer clear. Have you heard from Bailey?"

"She called around noon. Nothing to report yet on the Avengers, but I didn't expect anything until after classes start. She discovered something interesting about the paintball team at SFA. It's made up entirely of students enrolled in ROTC."

"That fits," said Lou. "A lot of veterans take up the sport. Future military officers could benefit from playing war without using real bullets. I bet those guys from A&M's team are in the corps of cadets."

"They are. Bailey keeps up with them on Facebook."

Lou changed the subject. "Doesn't she have a doctor's appointment coming up with the burn specialist in Houston?"

Fen loaded a worn pair of brown boots. "Candy got her appointment changed to this coming Saturday. She's driving to Houston by herself in her new ride."

Lou raised her eyebrows. "The baby bird is trying out her new wings."

He huffed a scoffing breath. "That bird's been in full flight for a long time. She matured fast in Houston before she moved here. Part of that process included learning to drive a variety of makes and models after hot-wiring them."

"Why does that not surprise me?"

Lou didn't press for details, so he changed the conversation. "What's the fallout from your last article?"

"The owner of the Lufkin paper didn't want to print it until the local television station picked up the story. Along with my story he also printed a complete but poorly worded denial from Leroy Clover, the so-called spokesman for the Avengers. I still believe someone else is behind the curtain, pulling the levers with that group of misfits."

"Any idea who?"

Lou moved into the shadow of the camper shell so she wasn't squinting into the sun. "I received an anonymous phone call after I got home saying the actual leader is Pete Crane."

"The guy who almost lost his face to a bomb in his mailbox? That seems unlikely."

"That's what the guy told me. He sounded like Leroy Clover trying to disguise his voice, but it could have been some other hick. I told Chuck about the call. He's contacting Lieutenant Morse to get her to trace it."

Lou offered a sardonic smile. "Put Leroy on your list of people to talk to. I think you'll agree he's lacking in the leadership department."

Fen grunted what could be interpreted as an affirmation, or a rejection of her suggestion. He then asked, "What's your next step?"

Lou snapped her fingers. "I almost forgot. I have all the names of the Avengers team members."

This was good news. His mind spun with possibilities of how he could proceed with the investigation. It shouldn't take him long to discover the actual leader of the Avengers. Before he chased that wild rabbit, a question came to him that Lou could answer. "I thought everyone in Angelina County had their lips sewn shut. How did you get someone to talk?"

"I had to look outside the state. Remember when the guys from A&M talked about how the Avengers cheated when they won the tournament in Missouri? I did what any good reporter would do and searched until I found who put on the tournament. They required the names of all the participants. The lady I talked to said she normally wouldn't give out that type of information, but the Avengers didn't make any friends in the Ozarks, especially after they dug a pit which resulted in a broken leg."

Lou took a breath. "I'll email the list to you."

Lost in thought, Fen nodded his appreciation, then asked, "What's your next step?"

"The ball's in your court, Professor Fen. I'm staying away from pine trees until I cover the tournament. Since Texas is a constitutional carry state, I might buy a pistol and have it on my hip when I come. That should give the guy who abducted me second thoughts about a repeat performance."

This was a turnaround for Lou. "I thought you fought your battles with paper and ink."

"I didn't say I'd put bullets in it."

Fen shook his head. "Think twice about it. If you're going to carry, go through a training class, and be ready to use it."

Lou tucked her hair behind her right ear, a habit she had before asking a probing question. "What about you? Are you still committed to not carrying a pistol?"

He didn't take the bait. "I'll keep the bad guys guessing about that one. I'm still a certified police officer."

She took a step toward him. "That should have expired by now. How are you...?" Her words trailed off. "Even though it goes against my training as a reporter, I'm learning not to ask questions when it involves Chuck, Candy, and you."

"You should probably add Bailey to that group."

A box containing tubes of paint and brushes went in next, followed by a large suitcase. "That's the last of what I'm taking. I hope to come home some weekends but can't promise it. I'll have access to a nice art studio at the university and I'm excited about finding locations to paint. The lakes and rivers in that neck of the woods have me itching to put some variety in my works. The Angelina River flows into Sam Rayburn Reservoir in Angelina County. I'm hoping it warms up so I can work outside."

"What about your home and land? Four thousand acres and this mini-mansion is a lot to leave alone."

He waved away the question. "Thelma and Sam are here to run things."

Lou took a step toward her car and turned around. "You're not fooling me. You'll stay close to Bailey to make sure she stays out of mischief."

He grinned. "You and she have a lot in common. You're both good at stirring up trouble, but you're right. I'll watch out for her the best I can without blowing our cover. These next few weeks have the potential to be busy. It won't be easy keeping tabs on her, teaching classes, painting, and trying to find out who kidnapped you."

"The last part shouldn't be too hard. Your search will start and end with the leader of the Avengers. If he didn't do it, he ordered it."

Fen slapped his hands together in a gesture of having finished a task. "I hope you're right, but I have an uneasy feeling this will be more complicated than you think."

Thelma came from the house carrying a white plastic grocery bag and a thermos. After exchanging a word of greeting with Lou, she handed Fen her parting gifts. "I packed you some fresh vegetables and fruit to munch on and some unsweetened tea. I know you'll eat everything that's bad for you from now until you come home, but I won't have your hard arteries on my conscience."

Fen peeked in the bag. She not only had packed Ziplock bags of vegetables, but also several dozen cookies. When his eyebrows rose in an expression of delight, she cut him off before he could eke out a syllable.

"Those cookies are for Bailey. I thought she could share them with the girls in the dorm. She's such a loner she needs something to help her make friends."

"I'll make sure she gets them."

Thelma gave him a hard stare. "Six dozen cookies are in that bag. There better be seventy-two delivered to Bailey. You have a key to her SUV. Leave the bag in the driver's seat as soon as you get to town. It's move-in day for the students that didn't go through new student orientation and she's expecting a text from you as soon as you get there. I'd better not get a call saying you snatched some of her cookies."

Some battles are worth fighting and others you let slide. Next stop? The bakery in town. He hadn't wanted cookies until Thelma told him he couldn't have any.

The delay only cost him a few minutes. Once he reached highway speed after clearing Springdale's city limit, he reached into the white paper sack and withdrew the first of three cookies. The jangle of his phone came as he examined the large chunks of chocolate poking up like tiny mountains. He balanced the cookie on his thigh and pressed the incoming call icon on the truck's computer screen.

"Bailey. You beat me to the punch. I was going to call when I made it to Centerville."

"If you're just now leaving, I might pass you going the other direction."

"What are you talking about?"

The sound of a car door slamming came through the truck's speaker and the background noise dissipated. "I can't stay here. I'd rather be in a jail cell than with the girl they stuck me with."

He didn't know if he should breathe a sigh of relief or explore how serious she was about leaving college before classes started. Bailey continued before he could form a sentence.

"This girl is straight out of a movie about a rich girl who goes to college to join a sorority so she can be around snobs like her. Everything from her fingernails to her highlighted hair is fake. All she can talk about is going through Rush, whatever that is, and pledging her life to some sort of girls' club. I finally picked up that she was calling the various sororities by Greek letters. She talked nonstop about the sorority she wants to join and called herself a legacy. It's like she's from a different planet. If that wasn't enough, she rattled off the pros and cons of all the men's fraternities, like they were the only guys on earth."

He tried to respond, but Bailey's need to vent cut him off. "That dorm room isn't big enough for one person, let alone two. Her parents pulled a U-Haul behind her mother's shiny, new SUV and unloaded enough junk to furnish a two-bedroom apartment. Apparently, my last-minute registration upset their plans. They were told their precious Allison wouldn't have a roommate and paid extra for it." She took a breath. "That's fine with me. If one of us has to go, I'll gladly volunteer."

Fen glanced down at the cookie calling him to take a bite. He mentally told it to be quiet and focused on Bailey. "Tell me what you've done to solve this problem."

Her words came like the crack of a whip. "Didn't you hear me? I'm packing and coming home. The only things I have left in the room are my clothes."

"Did you call Candy and have her try to help you?"

"Uh... no. I didn't think of that."

"Call her. If things don't change by the time I get there, we'll implement Plan B."

Even though Plan B didn't exist, another thought came to him. "What about Allison's parents? What's her mother doing about the mix-up?"

"There's a girl who lives at the end of the hall who's supposed to help us. I think they call her an R.A."

"Resident Assistant," said Fen.

"Whatever," said Bailey with disgust. "Allison's mother lit into her like a hungry cat on a grasshopper. The last I saw of them the R.A. was crying and the other two left to talk to someone else. I had enough of the drama queens and started loading my SUV with canvases and paints."

Fen could see in his mind's eye how this would play out, and he believed the problem would soon fade to a memory. The one thing Bailey didn't need to do was overreact. His plan for getting information depended on her.

A course of action came to him. "Here's what I want you to do. Call Candy. She'll know what to do. Then clear out the rest of your belongings. Get out your sketch pad and pencils and draw a flattering caricature of Allison with a cloud above her head like she's thinking. Inside the cloud put the Greek letters of the sorority she wants to join. Give it to her."

"Why should I do that?"

"It's called targeted advertising. You're applying for work from Allison and her mother. They'll remember you for not throwing a fit and insisting half the room was yours. Think like a businesswoman. You'll deliver a quality work of art that may lead to commissions. Remember what happened when you drew the two guys from A&M?"

A blast of breath came through the phone's speaker. "Where am I supposed to sleep tonight? It could blow our covers if I crashed on the couch in your apartment."

"Let's take this one step at a time. Call Candy, then knock out the sketch before you go back in to clear out your clothes. I'll be there in a couple of hours. I have cookies for you from Thelma."

"What kind?"

"Six dozen. Various kinds. All homemade. She wants you to share them with the other girls in your dorm."

"But I don't have a room."

"You will. Enrollment always decreases after the fall semester. There's a room for you somewhere on that campus."

Uncertainty filled her voice. "If you say so, but if I don't have a room tonight, I'm not sticking around this place, no matter how pretty it is and how much I'm looking forward to painting the river and forests."

"Start sketching. You'll see. This is a minor problem that will soon be nothing but an experience you'll laugh about."

The three chocolate chunk cookies weighed heavily on his stomach when he received the text from Bailey as he drove through Davy Crockett National Forest.

In same dorm. Top floor. Room by myself. Leave cookies where Thelma told you to.

A wide smile separated his lips. With the crisis averted, he had his spy in place. Classes would begin on Monday morning. He'd be teaching one class and mentoring students a few hours a day. Plenty of time to discover the leader of the Avengers. This investigation was working out to be nine parts vacation and one part investigation.

He heard a voice in his head say 'The best laid plans of mice and men...'

Chapter Nine

Although Fen's first and only class of the day didn't begin until 10:00 a.m., he parked in the faculty parking lot and arrived at the fine arts building more than an hour early. He enjoyed and appreciated the beauty of the manicured campus that boasted flora and fauna of all kinds as well as towering pine trees. With student enrollment topping out around fourteen thousand, the campus buzzed with activity. A wide variety of undergraduate and advanced degrees existed, but the Forestry Department held the prize for the most prestige, offering an internationally recognized doctoral program.

It had been two decades since his shadow had darkened the door of a university classroom. There was something both familiar and disquieting about being there. He arrived at the office of the head of the art department and knocked.

"Enter," came the woman's voice.

He complied and asked, "Dr. Bell?"

A woman who appeared to be in her late thirties glanced up. "You must be Fen Maguire."

"That's me. Reporting for duty." He regretted the levity in his voice as soon as the words left his mouth.

Dr. Bell frowned and refocused on whatever she was working on without extending an invitation for him to sit. He took the time afforded by the awkward silence to study the woman. His initial estimation of her age seemed accurate enough. What set her apart was over-size eyeglasses. Two perfectly round lenses of exceptional thickness seemed to cover half her face and magnified her eyes to unfortunate proportions. He couldn't imagine a more unflattering choice.

The professor tore herself away from whatever held her attention. "I'll be frank with you, Mr. Maguire. I find your formal training to be inadequate and your reputation as an artist to be overrated."

Fen didn't respond, but Dr. Bell had more to say.

"I don't take kindly to the administration foisting you upon me without so much as the courtesy of consultation. I've had to revise my schedule, but what really concerns me is the students who signed up for the class you'll teach. My fear is they will waste a semester. Are you prepared to follow the syllabus?"

She didn't give him time to answer. "I insist the students in Introduction to Painting with Acrylics come away with a thorough knowledge of art theory. It lays the foundation for their future classes."

Again, Fen didn't respond. She held a pen in a shaking left hand and looked away instead of locking her gaze on him. Her words seemed scripted, even though she delivered them with conviction. An invader had come to her fiefdom, and she intended to protect her turf. It occurred to him she might be insecure in her position.

"Well?" she asked. "Don't you have anything to say?"

He spoke in an even tone, not wanting to provoke her on the first day. "I have the syllabus, but I haven't picked up the textbooks yet. Amazon didn't offer them and the bookstore couldn't ship them in time."

She stared at him. "If you haven't read the texts, you're not prepared to teach my ten o'clock class. This means I'll have to step in for you."

Fen straightened his posture. "You've made it clear you believe I'm not qualified to instruct a college-level class and you're probably right. This doesn't negate the fact that I'm a very good professional artist who's here at the request of the university. You're stuck with me for this semester, and this semester only. I suggest we work together to come up with a plan to appease the administration, allow me to fulfill my contract, and provide the students with an experience that combines formal education with practical application."

For the first time, she looked at him without turning away. It was like he'd thrown her a life preserver that might keep her afloat. "What do you suggest?"

"You teach the classroom portion and I'll cover the studio and field trips. The reasons I agreed to come here are to help students paint and continue to develop my skills in a unique environment."

Hesitation slipped into Dr. Bell's words and voice. "I'm not sure the dean will agree to this arrangement."

Fen asked, "Do you know my background?"

"You were a highway patrolman and then a sheriff. Otherwise, landscape paintings are your claim to fame."

He nodded. "Have you ever heard of the Miranda Warning?"

"Isn't that the one you hear on television and in movies about not having to talk to the police without a lawyer?"

This time, a smile accompanied his nod. "I'm going to pretend the dean is a cop and I'm under arrest. I don't plan on telling her anything about us agreeing to do something unorthodox. We're two professionals who made a slight modification to a rushed plan that will better serve the students."

Dr. Bell's magnified eyes shifted from left to right and back again as she considered. She stood and extended her right hand to shake. "I'm still mad at her for not consulting me, so I'll return her lack of communication with some of my own. My name is Beverly, but I'm Bev to my friends."

"I look forward to the semester, Bev. My full name is James Fenimore Maguire. If you call me James or Fenimore, I won't answer you."

"All right, Fen." She looked at her phone. "There's still enough time for me to show you the studio. Are you ready to see your new home?"

"More than ready. Don't expect to find me anywhere else in this building."

Bev circled her desk. "That's good, because you don't have an office. I planned on running you off."

The art studio proved to be smaller than what he expected, with about twenty easels set up in a circle around a raised platform. Bev explained, "We primarily use this room for painting the human form. It requires students to capture the subject from different angles, which, as you know, is challenging."

"I know well what a challenge the human body poses." He looked at her. "No pun intended. Miscalculating the size and shape of any part can turn the painting into a caricature. That's why I choose to emphasize the landscape in my works."

"Are you saying you sacrifice quality for quantity?"

"Most of the time." He looked and listened for a response that came in a couple of seconds.

"You disappoint me. I believe an artist should paint at the direction of their muse without regard to financial remuneration."

He looked at her. "That's not what the masters did. Most

survived by painting what their patrons wanted. It's somewhat different today, but financial reality still enters the equation. My landscapes are popular and they sell at a price that satisfies me. Portraits aren't very much in vogue these days. If things turn around, I'll tell my muse to follow the money into painting old successful men, beautiful rich women, and cherubic children."

Her laugh had a nice alto tone to it. "You sound like my husband. He's a professor in the business department. I don't know how we've stayed together, but I can't imagine life any other way." She turned to face a door and took a step toward it. "This way to the other studio."

They entered, and it was half again larger than the first room. Easels with fresh canvases dotted the floor in irregular rows. This was what he'd imagined. It would be where he'd spend the majority of his time painting, giving students pointers, and the occasional honest critique. He also looked forward to hours of getting so absorbed in a scene that his mind could roam and speak to him about the crimes he was there to solve. Something of a mysterious alchemy happened when brush strokes and clues blended. The thought of Bev and her husband came to mind. Opposites, but the differences somehow worked together.

His pondering came to an abrupt end when Bev said, "Look at the time. It won't do if I'm late for my first class of the semester. Stop by the office after my class and I'll give you keys to the building and studios."

In the room's solitude, he considered what he needed to do for the rest of the day. The university would supply all the canvases and supplies he needed. A good thing, since he'd already set up his easel in the living room of his apartment with the only blank canvas he brought.

This left him with the question of where to put the finished works he brought. Six figures in potential sales sat in the back of his truck, waiting for a thief with a screwdriver to come along, pry open the flip-up window to the camper shell, and make off for parts unknown. He decided to bring his works to the studio and leave them there until he and Bailey worked their first festival.

He arrived back from his second trip from the parking lot to find about twenty students and Bev looking at four of his paintings. Bailey was one of them.

Bev took over. "Everyone. If I can have your attention. This is Fen Maguire, the artist responsible for these works."

She turned to Fen. "I hope you don't mind, but the students insisted they see your works. I saw you leaving and told them I didn't think you'd brought anything in."

A man with his hair pulled back in a bun said, "I was late to class and saw you puffing your way into the building holding the paintings. I'm a journalism student, thinking about getting a minor in art. I recognized you from your picture that will run in the PINE LOG."

"The what?" asked Fen.

Three students answered at the same time. "The campus newspaper."

A wide-eyed girl of short stature moved in front of him. "Do you mind if we put these on easels?"

"Help yourself. In fact, there's a few more in my truck if anyone would like to get them for me. I have a trick knee that's protesting the coming change of weather." He looked at Bailey. "Young lady, you look trustworthy. Would you mind taking my keys and getting the remaining paintings out of my truck?"

Bailey held up her bandaged hand. "I'll unlock it, but I'm not supposed to carry anything heavy yet."

"Grab the keys," said bun-man. "Three or four of us will help you." He looked at Fen. "What kind of truck?"

Fen described it and the group was off.

Questions came at Fen fast and furious, evenly divided between what it took to produce high-quality works of art and the economics involved in selling them.

Bailey and crew returned with the balance of the works that soon found their way onto easels. At noon, Bev called a halt to the impromptu class. The students complained, but filed out of the studio, leaving only the two teachers. Once they were alone, Bev focused on a portrait he'd painted that captured only the eyes, eyebrows, and part of the nose of a man.

"That one I call *Grief*," he said.

"I can feel it," whispered Bev, in a tone reserved for funerals. It seemed she couldn't tear her gaze away from it. "I'd say you painted this by looking in a mirror."

He pursed his lips to keep a quivering chin from betraying him.

She turned away and dragged her hand across his shoulders as she passed behind him. Approaching the door, she turned. "I was wrong. You can paint anything you put your mind to. I'm glad you're here—and incredibly envious of your talent."

He examined the paintings for another few minutes then stacked them in a corner. It was time to move on with the investigation that brought him to East Texas. He took out his phone and called Lieutenant Morse, but had to leave a message. "Angie, Fen Maguire. I believe I know who the real leader of the Avengers is. Also, I need a small boat."

Chapter Ten

The day started in the usual manner, with coffee and time with Sally, only without her ashes in front of him. He also thought of Bailey then checked the time. His first inclination was to send her a text to make sure she was on the road to Houston for her doctor's appointment. Considering her streak of independence, he put his phone on the coffee table. Let the little bird fly.

Finishing a sketch took up the next hour before he loaded an easel into the back of his truck, along with a couple of fresh canvases and a new sketch pad. A box containing pencils, tubes of paint, and brushes went in next. Not wanting to face another breakfast of bagels and cream cheese, he found a coffee shop on the main drag that promised the best omelets in town. It occurred to him he'd have to try every restaurant within the city limits to verify each one's boast.

Highway 7 took him west out of Nacogdoches, toward the Angelina River and the county by the same name. Lieutenant Angie Morse set their rendezvous for nine thirty. No need to be in too big of a hurry on this cool Saturday morning. By the time he arrived, she had a twelve-foot-long aluminum boat already in the water.

"Good morning, Professor Maguire."

He shot her a smile but didn't respond to the unearned title. "This boat looks perfect. It's big enough for me to put all my painting supplies in. Thanks."

Angie stood facing the sun and squinted as she looked up at him. "The Angelina isn't near the river she was before they made Sam Rayburn Reservoir. It's not like the Brazos River you're used to. Watch out for shallow spots, sand bars, and the occasional fallen tree." She glanced at the river and pointed. "I made sure there weren't any bodies in it before you got here."

"I appreciate that. The body I found last fall was enough to last me for quite a while." He lifted the window portion of the camper shell and dropped the tailgate. "How long will it take me to get where the paintball competition will take place?"

"It all depends on how comfortable you are with a twenty-horsepower motor. I'd say twenty minutes. You'll recognize it by a wooden dock on the Nacogdoches side."

"Is that land privately owned?"

She took a sip from an insulated cup. "One of the richest families in this part of the state owns it. Their crop is long-leaf pine trees and they encourage people who carry a badge to use it for hunting, camping, and picnics. They're also huge supporters of the university, so there's no problem with you putting in at the dock. You could have driven in on a logging road, but you'd need a map and a guide to where you're going."

As she spoke, he pulled everything he intended to take onto the tailgate. "I'm looking for places to take my students to paint landscapes. Would the dock be a suitable location?"

"The river widens out there, so it should be a great place." She tilted her head to one side. "What else are you up to?"

He liked Angie. She thought several steps ahead and wasn't

afraid to ask questions. He could see her wearing captain bars in the not-too-distant future. "I chose that location because it's across the river from the upcoming paintball competition. That's next Saturday. I thought the Avengers might practice today."

Angie put her travel mug down and grabbed his box of supplies. He took the easel, and they walked side-by-side toward the boat. She spoke again when they reached the water's edge. "From what I've heard, the Avengers practice every weekend. I'm not sure how close they'll be to the river today."

He put the easel into the boat and took the box from Angie. "I'm mainly looking for a remote place to bring students to paint. If I happen to see and talk to any of the Avengers, it will be icing on the cake."

With all the equipment packed, he turned to face her. "What do you think about my theory of Chet Lowe being the behind-the-scenes leader of the Avengers?"

"You may be onto something." There wasn't much conviction in her words. She added, "I ran criminal records on all the members. Lowe has three arrests for domestic violence. Some of the others have worse records."

"True," said Fen. "But not when you consider his juvenile and military records."

Her head jerked toward him. "How did you get his juvenile record? They're supposed to be sealed."

He shifted his gaze toward the river. "If you don't know, it's for a reason. Keep in mind I can get by with things you can't because I'm a private citizen."

Instead of pressing him, she asked, "When do you need me back here?"

He looked at the puffy clouds meandering across a canvas of blue. "I plan on staying until dusk if the weather holds."

"The rain's not supposed to set in until tomorrow. I'll be here at five-thirty unless something big breaks loose."

He thought about all the times he'd made plans with his late wife, only to have them interrupted by a phone call from dispatch or one of his deputies. He swallowed the memory and stepped into the boat.

The journey up river revealed a greater variety of trees than he expected. Oak, hickory, sweetgum, dogwood, and the occasional cypress were a few he could identify. That didn't include the wide variety of bushes that hugged the river banks. Recent moderate rains caused the river to flow at a decent rate, which meant the sandbars Angie warned him about shouldn't be a problem.

The motor chugged at a modest pace until he reached the dock about half an hour later. The river widened, as described, and a weathered wooden dock extended out from a natural cove formed by a creek that stayed dry until a decent rain motivated it to flow. He tied the boat aft, then fore, and scanned the bank. Unlike the steep banks he'd seen along the way, the land rose gently from the river on both banks and was clear of trees and thick brush. He looked across the river and thought to himself that this would be the perfect spot to bring his students. Plenty of room to spread out on the bank and few obstructions. They would have a clear view to establish a horizon line with the tops of pines in the distance.

With the easel set up, he spent the first thirty minutes making a pencil sketch and taking photos. He'd need them when he added details to the oil-on-canvas he saw in his mind's eye.

A shout from across the river interrupted his concentration. He abandoned his sketch pad and walked to the end of the dock. He didn't make out the first words from the man hollering at him, so he made a megaphone of his hands and hollered, "Good morning."

The man wore camo from head to foot. If he wasn't standing in an opening, he'd blend in perfectly with his surroundings. The man hollered back, "Who are you?"

Fen didn't intend to have a long-distance shouting match, so he cupped his hands behind his ears, giving the signal that he couldn't hear the man, even though he could. He megaphoned his hands again and shouted. "I'll come over where I can hear you."

The motor came to life on the first pull. In no time, he eased the bow into the mud of the far bank. The man held a pump shotgun, and carried a pistol in a camo holster strapped to his thigh. Neither weapon shot paintballs. He wore full tactical gear, had a thick salt-and-pepper beard, and wasn't smiling as he descended the bank with the sure-footedness of a deer coming to water.

"Who are you, and what are you doing here?" demanded the man.

Fen knew better than to say what crossed his mind. "The name's Fen. I'm an artist." He pointed across the river. "I'm sketching a scene for my next painting."

The man's words came with absolute conviction. "You're a liar. I saw you taking pictures of this land. What team sent you to scout the competition?"

Fen held up his hands to show he posed no danger. "I don't have a clue what you're talking about. I'm a teacher in the art department at SFA and I'm looking for remote locations where I can bring students. The perspective from the clearing on the other side of the dock is perfect. The photos will allow me to remember details for the painting. I'll be bringing about twenty students at a time to paint the dock and this side of the river."

"The heck you will. Find another spot that isn't near our property."

"Don't worry. We'll drive in and not come by boat. We won't set foot on this side of the river."

The man took a step forward and tickled the safety on the shotgun. "You must not have heard me. It'll be bad for your health if you keep coming around here. The same goes for anyone from the college."

"University," said Fen. "A college doesn't offer advanced degrees."

The man clicked the safety off. "Interrupt me one more time and there's going to be an unfortunate accident."

"Sure. I just wanted to let you know who I am and what to expect across the river." He smiled. "By the way, you have no right to tell me I can't bring students across the river to paint."

The barrel of the shotgun rose until it pointed at his chest. Fen swallowed. "Why don't I show you my faculty identification card? Would that be enough for you to point that shotgun somewhere else?"

"I won't give you an answer until I see it."

"It's in my wallet, back pocket of my jeans. I'm going to reach for it with these two fingers." He held up his thumb and forefinger while he folded the other three fingers on his right hand into a tight ball.

"If anything but a wallet comes out, you'll be food for the fish."

With slow, deliberate movements, Fen brought the wallet around, opened it, and held up the identification card. The shotgun pointed away from his chest. The click of the safety sounded almost as loud as Fen's heartbeat.

"All right, you're a useless art teacher. That changes nothing. Find another place to paint."

Fen considered how to respond. He needed to get as much information from this man as he could, but how to go about it without bloodshed? Especially his.

Chapter Eleven

The diameter of the shotgun barrel looked like a small cannon. The answer of how to get out of the predicament came, but Fen didn't like it. He needed to act fast before he talked himself out of it.

"It occurs to me that you know my name, but I don't know yours." He returned his wallet to his back pocket. When he brought his hand around, it held the nine-millimeter Glock pistol he'd stuffed in his back waistband. The business end pointed at a spot between the camo-man's eyes.

"Don't think about it!" shouted Fen in the voice he learned to use in Highway Patrol Academy.

The man's gaze began with eyelids wide and soon narrowed in a way that reminded him of a look from a venomous snake. "You just signed your death warrant, mister."

"That's big talk. Do you know this trigger only requires six pounds of pressure for your life to end? The first thing you're going to do is gently lay that shotgun on the bow of this boat."

The man's eyes darted from left to right. A twisted smile

lifted one corner of his mouth and he lowered the shotgun toward the top rail of the boat.

"Stop!" shouted Fen. "Use only your right hand, and it better not be anywhere near the trigger. The left hand goes to the top of your head. As soon as the shotgun is resting on aluminum, your right hand will join the left, up top. Try for the Sig Sauer strapped to your leg and things will get messy."

The man huffed, "Like I said, you're not a college teacher or artist."

The shotgun lay across the bow of the boat. So far, so good.

"Slowly, bring only your left hand down and take out the Sig with thumb and forefinger. I don't think you're stupid enough to try anything, but I'm not taking any chances. Close your eyes tight until I tell you to open them."

The man spoke as he complied. "You're too well trained. You must be a veteran or a cop."

Fen ignored the bait. "Using only your finger and thumb, pitch the pistol over your shoulder, far as you can. Make a good throw and with a little luck it won't land barrel down."

He did as he was told and opened his eyes after the pistol landed in a bush on top of the bank. "You planned this all along. Was it A&M or those ROTC idiots from SFA who sent you?"

"Take four steps back."

He glared until Fen gave his next command. "I know you have a Ka-Bar somewhere on you. Take it out and throw it toward your pistol. Remember, it's only a fool who brings a knife to a gun fight."

Once more, metal rattled against the underbrush.

"You probably have a butterfly knife or two hidden on you somewhere, but I'm not in the mood to strip search you this morning." Fen changed his voice to something more friendly while lowering his point of aim to a place no man would want to be shot. "I don't think it's fair that you know my name and I don't know yours."

"It's Peter Pan."

Fen chuckled. "More like one of the lost boys. Perhaps I should reconsider that strip search." He paused. "No, I have a better idea. This phone takes excellent pictures and videos. I bet the campus newspaper at SFA would love to print a story about how an art instructor disarmed a guy who pointed a shotgun at him. They'll enjoy reading about how you told me I couldn't bring students to paint landscapes. Think about your reputation when the video goes viral and the local television station picks up the story."

The man's darting eyes betrayed him. Fen allowed the passage of time to solidify the threat. Seconds ticked by. Everyone feared something. Bullies feared embarrassment and public humiliation more than jail or physical pain. Camo-man ran a hand down his beard. "All right. My name is Chet Lowe. I drive a pulpwood truck. Satisfied?"

"Almost. What's with the gear and you accusing me of scouting for A&M or SFA?"

He threw a thumb over his shoulder. "The property behind me is where we'll hold a paintball tournament next weekend. My team never loses."

Fen nodded as he reached for the shotgun. "Nice to meet you, Mr. Lowe." He lifted the shotgun with his left hand, swung the barrel over the side of the boat, and jammed it downward into thick mud.

"Hey! Why'd you do that?"

The question didn't deserve an answer, but Fen provided one anyway. "You called me a liar. That means you need to learn a lesson about manners. I'm going to spend the day across the river sketching and I'm coming back some other day with students." Fen took a deep breath. "Out of respect for you and your team, it won't be during the tournament. All you had to do was ask instead of pointing that twelve gauge at me."

"Are you finished?"

"Not yet. I'm going to take a photo of you unarmed and email it to myself explaining what happened here today. If anything happens to me, expect a visit from the police. They'll search my computer and you'll have a lot of explaining to do."

"Anything else?"

"Be sure to clean the mud out of your shotgun before you use it."

Chet rolled his eyes, showing the advice wasn't necessary.

Now that Fen had the man over a barrel, he said. "The Avengers have been getting some bad press lately. A bomb seriously injured one of your members, and then there's the abduction of a woman reporter. I also read something about loggers having to pay to keep their trucks from being damaged."

"Those stories are a pack of lies. That reporter and the cops can't prove any of it."

"What about the abduction? Did she make that up, too?"

Chet didn't hesitate. "All I know is, it wasn't me or any of my men."

Fen shook his head, showing he didn't believe the denial. "You'll need to do better than that if the cops come knocking on your door."

"All right. I'll give you a couple of possibilities. First, she arranged it with a team we're competing against. They took her into the woods, dropped her off, and blamed it on us."

The absurdity of the story earned a laugh. "That sounds like something Peter Pan would make up. Try again."

He gave a half-hearted smirk. "You're right. The simplest explanation is she's a smart woman who knows how to create a story that catches people's interest. She planned and carried out her own abduction because her story was too weak. All she needed was one accomplice to take her to the woods and drop her off. Everyone knows if reporters don't have a story, they make something up. She's a has-been that couldn't cut it in Dallas."

Fen shrugged. "I like that story better than the first one." He rested his pistol on his thigh. "What about the bomb in the mailbox?"

The delay in responding gave Fen the answer he needed as much as the lie that followed it. "Pete must have been experimenting. I told him we play by the rules, but he wanted to make sure we kept winning every tournament."

Movement on the raised bank caught Fen's attention. Another man appeared; this one didn't carry a weapon and looked much younger. "Dad, the rest of the guys are looking for you."

Fen and Chet traded glances that communicated an unspoken agreement that no further embarrassment would befall the father. The pistol found a home in his jacket pocket as Fen turned to start the outboard motor and back out of the mud. He'd leave the leader of the Avengers to either tell the truth to his son or tell another lie.

After reaching the relative safety of the opposite bank, it seemed he'd entered another world. This one didn't contain lies, schemes, or aggression. He sat on a log and took up sketching where he'd left off. Long ago, he'd mastered the ability to create and also meditate deeply on solving crimes at the same time. To do so he had to lose himself in a painting. Sketching was the first step in creating a professional painting, so he set his mind to focus solely on capturing what nature was showing him.

Noon came and went, and by two thirty, he had six completed sketches from different angles. In his seventh sketch, he focused on the foreground, especially the dock. When thoughts shifted back to Chet Lowe, his pencil moved without effort. He'd reached a state of flow. It wasn't as deep as when he mixed paints and applied colors to canvas, but it revealed some things. By the time he finished the sketch, he believed Chet Lowe had planted the paint bomb in Pete Crane's mailbox. The hard part would come next: proving it.

Time had no meaning in the flow state. When he came out of it, he looked at his phone and realized he needed to pack his equipment and return to where Angie waited for him. The tyranny of time was upon him as he rushed to load his supplies. When he stepped with his right foot into the boat, slack in the lines caused the vessel to shift. The all-too-familiar sound of a snap echoed against the aluminum as his knee buckled. Pain overwhelmed all thoughts as he sprawled across the aluminum seat and struck his head on the far top rail. White dots appeared in his vision as his hand went instinctively to check for blood. Only a trickle, so he focused on the pain in his knee. He knew he'd spend the next week shuffling around on crutches.

The white spots in his vision disappeared as the pain from two locations alternated between extreme discomfort to pulsing agony and back again. It took a half dozen awkward pulls on the starter rope to get the motor to catch. By the time Angie's truck and trailer came into view, he'd had his fill of the hard aluminum seat and the drone of the outboard motor. At least she'd backed the trailer into the water. It took him two tries to get the boat centered and far enough up on the carpet-covered skids.

Angie secured the boat enough to get it out of the water. Then came the hard part: climbing out with only one good leg.

"What happened to you?" asked Angie when she examined the lump and dried blood on his face.

He spoke through gritted teeth. "Boating accident. The

head's not serious, but my trick knee went out on me again. It's going to be sketchy getting from this boat to the ground. From where I sit, it looks like fifty feet in the air."

"Do you need paramedics?"

He shook his head. "The last time I did something like this, they laughed so hard they dropped me. It's going to be awkward, but I think all you'll need to do is get my knee brace out of the back seat of my truck. As long as I can stabilize it, I won't do any more damage."

She brought the metal brace and he strapped it on over his jeans. Then came the awkward process of laying belly-down on the seat, having Angie lift his feet above the rail and him pushing backward until his body folded over the side. He kept pushing until both feet found solid ground. Standing brought new flashes of pain.

"Will it help if you put your arm over my shoulders and use me as a crutch?"

"I'll use the crutches in the back of my truck, if you can bring them to me."

Once he opened the driver's door, it was time to explain the next part of the process. "Don't be surprised if I scream when I do my next trick. I need to pull myself into the driver's seat by grabbing the steering wheel. My right leg will stick straight out."

"How will you drive like that?"

"That's when the screaming starts. I'll unlock the brace and allow gravity to bend my knee. Once it's bent, and I stop crying, I'll be able to maneuver it out of the way and operate the accelerator and brake with my left foot."

Angie shook her head. "You need a knee replacement."

"I'm warming up to the idea."

"How long will you be out of commission?"

"The loudness of the pop is how I judge these episodes.

This one sounded like splitting firewood with an ax. I'll be on strong pain meds for several days, so don't expect me to make sense if you call." He closed his eyes as a fresh spasm of pain overcame him.

"Are you sure you're safe to drive?"

He ignored the question. "I need you to find out everything you can about Chet Lowe. He's the leader of the Avengers. I'm convinced he planted the paint bomb in the mailbox. Unless I'm mistaken, Pete Crane was trying to take over the team."

"Are you sure?"

He gave the short version of how both of them looked down the barrels of weapons that morning and Chet's responses to his questions when Fen had the upper hand. Angie chuckled when he told her about the photos and email he sent to himself.

"I'll have to remember that trick if I'm ever in a similar situation."

"Looking down the barrel of a twelve gauge isn't the most comforting thing I've ever done. In fact, this was my first time."

She tilted her head and narrowed her gaze. "I thought you didn't carry a pistol."

"Today was the first time since I turned in my sheriff's badge. That little voice in my head told me going into the woods unarmed with people who play war games wasn't a smart thing to do."

Reaching down, he unlocked the brace... and screamed.

Chapter Twelve

Fen spent two miserable days icing his knee and popping pills. Bailey returned from Houston safe and sound, with good news from her surgeon. The skin grafts were healing better than expected. They replaced the sling and bandages with a cloth glove. As long as she didn't try to pick up anything weighing more than a paintbrush, she could start using her left hand again.

Late Monday afternoon, he received another phone call from her. "How's the knee?"

"Better." It wasn't much of a lie as he looked down at yet another ice pack. "I'll be able to hobble to the studio tomorrow, but I'm not sure how long I'll stay."

"Are you still taking those pills that make you sound like you downed a bottle of tequila?"

He focused on a plastic bottle of ibuprofen on the coffee table and muted the television. "Only the over-the-counter stuff. How were classes today?"

"Intro to Business was good. English 101 stinks, and Art

History was boring. I went to the studio and worked on ears and noses for a couple of hours. A graduate student will be there tonight, so I'll try to finish my self-portrait after supper."

"How are you adjusting to life in the dorm?"

The hesitation told him she searched for an answer. "It's fine now that I'm living by myself."

"Can you name some of the girls up and down the hall from you?"

She let out a huff. "What kind of question is that?"

"One that tells me you don't like to make friends. Did you pass out the cookies Thelma sent?"

"I left some with Allison and her mom when I moved to the top floor."

He didn't want to press her too hard on meeting people. She was a self-avowed introvert in an environment that was as foreign to her as moving to a distant country. Coming out of her shell would come with time, so he waited for her to speak.

His eyebrows raised when she said, "There's a guy in art class who's coming on to me. I know what I want to tell him, but I'm afraid it'd get me expelled. How should I handle him?"

Fen cleared his throat to buy time. The best he could come up with was, "What guy?"

"The dark-haired guy with the man-bun named Skyler. You met him. He's majoring in journalism and asked me to cover the paintball tournament with him this coming Saturday. He said he needs someone who knows what they're doing to take pictures. What a crock. It doesn't take an artist to snap a few photos with today's phones."

Fen's thoughts went into high gear. "You should go. If not for your personal interest in the guy or the campus newspaper, then for me and Lou. I'll still be out of commission and I need a spy at the tournament. Lou's coming to town on Friday to write another story. She's still ticked off about being abducted. The guy who really leads the Avengers has a quick temper and isn't happy about the stories Lou wrote."

The repositioning of his leg brought a fresh stab of pain. He fought through it and continued speaking. "There's no telling what he might do if she backs him into a corner with a bunch of hard questions, especially if she's alone. He won't do anything in front of witnesses, but you know how she is when there's a story. Good judgment and caution get thrown to the wind."

A grumble came forth. "I'll do it, but only because it's Lou. There's something seriously wrong with skinny guys who wear their hair up like an old woman. It takes good abs and arms to pull off that look." She huffed again. "I doubt his real name is Skyler."

Fen ignored her comments, and said, "Thanks. I knew I could count on you. Go get something to eat, then paint until they kick you out. This case should be over by this time next week. That will give us both plenty of time to work and have an adequate selection to sell at the spring fairs."

"And for me to tell Skyler to find some other girl to bother."

The phone cut off and he couldn't help but smile. All that remained was to put the second half of his impromptu plan in place. This one might be trickier to pull off.

While still holding his phone, he instructed it to call Lou. She answered on the fourth ring. "I hear you did a good job on your knee this time."

"You heard right. I'll be on crutches for a week."

"Is Bailey helping you with meals?"

"I've been on a diet of pills and water until lunch today. One good thing about living in a college town is there are plenty of places to call that deliver." He looked on the coffee table at the remains of his late lunch in takeout containers.

"Lasagna and salad tastes pretty good after forty-eight hours of fasting."

He knew Lou wasn't one to express pity for a fixable problem. He moved on. "Did Chuck or Candy fill you in on my meeting with Chet Lowe?"

"Candy said you believe he's the leader of the Avengers. I went over my notes and think you're right. I can't wait to question him this weekend."

"Did she give you details of my encounter with Chet and how we traded pleasantries while taking turns looking down the barrels of each other's weapons?"

"What? No, she didn't."

He could see Lou in his imagination, reaching for a pen and her notebook.

"Wait. You don't carry a gun anymore."

"I did Saturday morning, and it came in handy."

"This will make a great lead-in to the story I write about the tournament. Give me every detail and don't leave anything out."

"Sorry," he said as one side of his mouth came up in a grin. "I guess the pain medicine still has me loopy. I already said too much."

"No, you don't, Fen Maguire. If I have to drive to Nacogdoches tonight and stomp on your knee, I'm getting that story. Better yet, I'll tell Thelma what you did to your knee and bring her with me. She'll get the bedroom and you'll sleep on the couch. How would you like her hovering over you until she decides you're healed?"

The thought sent an icy shiver through him. "You fight dirty. She'd probably stay on so she could helicopter over Bailey until the semester ended." This was going better than he expected. He'd hooked Lou into a position of bargaining with him. Next came the delicate part... negotiating an agreement.

"I tell you what," he said. "I'll give you half the story under two conditions. First, you can't print anything until after the police arrest Chet Lowe."

"And the second condition?"

"You keep a close watch over Bailey at the tournament. She's going to take photos with a reporter for the campus newspaper. He's sweet on her, but the feelings are one-way. I don't think he's ever interviewed anyone as dangerous as Chet Lowe, and I don't want anyone getting hurt."

She responded in the way he expected. "I don't like it. For one, I work alone and get exclusives. Speed is the lifeblood of any good newspaper story." She paused for several seconds. "I'll make an exception because it's Bailey, and only publish what goes on at the tournament. But," she said with emphasis. "I get all the details of your encounter with Chet—tonight."

A full smile replaced the half-smile of a few minutes ago. "It's a deal."

Lou followed every piece of information she received with questions. It took the better part of forty-five minutes for him to relay all the details of his trip up the Angelina and the dangerous encounter.

By the time he'd finished, Lou believed Mr. Lowe was suspect number one for the bombing and her abduction. Fen held back on agreeing with her on the abduction.

It took only a few seconds for him to summarize how he'd re-injured his knee. He purposefully omitted the details of traveling back down the Angelina and his ungraceful exit from the boat.

Lou responded with, "I know there's a lot you're not telling me, but I can get the details Friday night. I made hotel reservations earlier today. I'll stay in Nacogdoches."

Self-satisfaction came upon Fen as he considered the coup he'd accomplished. Bailey would come back from the tournament with current photos of the team members and she'd make sure Lou didn't do something stupid like walk into the woods with Chet Lowe to confront him. Conversely, Lou would monitor Bailey. Both would return to Nacogdoches with the one commodity he needed the most... information.

Lou ARRIVED at his apartment Friday afternoon after checking into the Fredonia Hotel in historic downtown Nacogdoches. It didn't surprise him that her first question had to do with the case and not the condition of his leg. It wasn't that she was hard-hearted, but pursuing stories was her one genuine passion.

He fed her addiction by saying, "I spoke with Angie Morse a little while ago. The sheriff will apply for an arrest warrant on Monday. He wanted to wait until after the Avengers won the tournament with their star player."

"Are you kidding?" asked Lou with disgust written all over her face.

Fen countered with, "Chet isn't a flight risk. Since he left the Army, East Texas is the center of his universe. The only time he leaves is to travel to a tournament."

"I'll never understand Angelina County. What's the real religion? Is it paintball, Friday night football games, or the churches on every other corner?"

He answered with a shrug and said, "Probably all three."

Lou scanned the modest one-bedroom apartment. "I've heard of people downsizing, but you've taken it to the extreme."

"I feel like somebody put me in a time machine and sent me back almost thirty years. The layout is almost identical to my apartment the last year I was in college, except that one had two bedrooms and there were four twin beds. Four guys crammed into one apartment. It was such a pigsty that Sally refused to come over."

"Can't say that I blame her."

Fen was on shaky ground emotionally after bringing up Sally, so he moved on. "What are you hungry for tonight?"

Lou didn't hesitate. "Lasagna. Ever since you mentioned it Monday, I've had a craving for good Italian food. College towns always have some of the best."

"I'll grab my coat and you can drive us to *Rossini's*."

It wasn't long before they arrived at a converted warehouse in an older section of town. Exposed brick walls and small tables topped with candles dripping wax down the sides of wine bottles gave the room a feel of entering a restaurant tucked away on a side street on the other side of the Atlantic. Soft violin music added to the atmosphere.

Lou nodded her approval and asked, "Do you eat here often?"

"First time, but this is where I ordered the deliveries. They cook their pizzas in a wood-fired oven. I'm not sure I've ever had better."

She shook her head. "It's lasagna for me tonight. I've been thinking about it all week."

After ordering a glass of wine, Lou asked, "How's Bailey?"

He looked over her shoulder as the young artist approached. "In three seconds, you can ask her yourself."

Lou almost knocked over her chair getting up too fast. Bailey squealed as the two women hugged a greeting. They separated and Lou gave her a head-to-toe stare. "College life agrees with you."

Bailey shrugged. "It's not as bad as I thought it would be. I can't paint as much as I'd like because of the other classes, but the studio is awesome."

Both women shifted their gaze to Fen, but Lou beat Bailey to the question. "I thought you and Bailey weren't to be seen together anywhere but in the art studio."

"Yeah," said Bailey. "What's up with that?"

"Sit down, and I'll tell you."

They did, and he rested his forearms on the white table-cloth. "The police have enough evidence to arrest and convict Chet Lowe of the bomb in the mailbox. It turns out the footprint they found at the crime scene matches one of his old boots. His wife gave him an alibi, but the D.A. thinks he can make the charges stick."

"What about him abducting me? Did the footprint Sam found match those boots?"

Fen nodded his head. "It's from the same boot. If they find it when they search his house, he'll be looking at two charges."

Bailey's eyes brightened. "That explains why you don't mind eating with us in public. The cops are finally doing their job."

Fen nodded. "One case solved for sure, and the other on Monday." He opened the menu and perused the selections. "All the locals needed was a little nudge and Lou gets the credit."

SATURDAY MORNING FLOWED into the afternoon. Fen's knee felt so much better that he abandoned the brace and the crutches. Truth be told, he could have gone to the tournament but didn't want to chance walking on uneven ground or tripping over a tree root. Instead, he went to the art studio and painted.

Two hours before dusk, his phone jangled a progression of notes informing him of an incoming call. Lieutenant Angie

Morse spoke in clipped sentences with the sound of a siren accompanying her words. "On my way to the tournament. We don't have to worry about arresting Chet Lowe. Someone shot him during the tournament."

"I'm on my way."

Chapter Thirteen

The trip from Nacogdoches to the backwoods of Angelina County gave Fen plenty of time to blame himself for not realizing the complexity of the cases and how they pointed to something much more serious. Now, a man was dead. Why didn't he realize Chuck and Candy sent him into a situation that was more than he believed it to be? The voice of self-condemnation accused and mocked him. He'd focused so much on Bailey getting the college experience that he'd lost sight of his primary job: identify the bad guys and provide evidence that would lead to convictions. AND put an end to a crime spree. To top it off, he'd not pressured local officials to arrest Chet Lowe when they should have. Justice shouldn't bow to sporting events.

He took in a deep breath of regret and mumbled, "If I'd done my job, Chet would be safe in a jail cell. He might have been a lousy man, but he didn't deserve a bullet."

An Angelina County sheriff's office SUV blocked the road leading to the one hundred acres owned by the Avengers. The deputy moved to Fen's window as he lowered it. "This road is closed."

"Fen Maguire. Lieutenant Morse is expecting me."

"Pull off the road in front of my vehicle and don't go anywhere until I talk to my sergeant."

Fen could have driven to Nacogdoches, and back by the time the deputy returned.

"All right, mister. You can go ahead, but don't stop until you get to another deputy. He'll tell you where you can and can't go. This entire area is an active crime scene. We don't want civilians contaminating evidence."

It took everything he had to choke back what came to mind, but he swallowed the words and proceeded until he saw Angie's black and white highway patrol SUV parked away from all the people and lights. She clambered out and met him at the driver's side window. "I didn't know if you still wanted to keep a low profile."

He nodded. "That's a good idea until we know more. Who did you tell them I am?"

"A professor at SFA, checking on the two journalism students. I vouched for you and told the sheriff you'd get any students out of here ASAP. Lou Cooper and that kid named Skyler are demanding answers and interviews. That doesn't fly very well with the sheriff."

"What about Bailey?"

"She's keeping a low profile so far, but I can tell the water in her kettle is close to boiling."

Fen looked into the dark forest as he sought a plan. "I don't want Lou in jail, but she needs to back off and let the forensic specialists do their job. Let's separate her from Bailey and both of them from Skyler. They'll start comparing notes and that makes for cross-contamination of statements."

He puffed out his cheeks. "Lou will kill me if she ever finds out, but given the circumstances, take her into custody for questioning. She's convinced Chet abducted her, and she may be right. That gives her plenty of motive for killing him, even though I'm positive she didn't. Get her away from here before she makes even more enemies."

"What about Bailey and Skyler?"

"I'll take Bailey and spend the rest of the evening getting her statement on what she saw and heard today."

Angie rested her forearm on the butt of her pistol. "And Skyler?"

"Bailey says he quotes the first amendment every chance he gets. My experience as a sheriff tells me the deputies aren't keen on college students quoting constitutional rights to them when they're trying to solve a murder. They'll feel better if they can arrest someone, even if it gets dismissed by noon tomorrow."

She glanced away for a moment. "Anything else?"

"I called Sam. He's on his way."

"You'd better call him back and tell him not to hurry. If the sheriff's men catch him anywhere on the hundred acres, it's jail for him."

Fen dismissed the warning. "I told him to stay outside the perimeter of the property until he heard from me. He'll park close to the dock on the Nacogdoches side of the river, cross it upstream, and work his way around the perimeter until he hits the river again. We need to know if anyone but players came onto the property."

"What about by boat?"

"He'll bring night-vision binoculars and check the riverbank. Believe me, he'll know if someone entered the property by boat. Let me know when the crime scene technicians and the deputies clear out. Once they're finished, I'll text Sam and he'll search the fence line."

Angie cocked her head. "He's a handy guy to have around."

"He makes me look smarter than I am."

She took a step back. "Let's rescue Lou and Bailey before they make us both look stupid."

———

HANDCUFFS CLICKED around Skyler's wrists as Fen and Angie approached. A second deputy told Lou to put her hands behind her back. Angie moved to intervene. Not wanting to interfere where he had no authority, Fen stood far enough away not to cause additional trouble, but close enough to hear. Bailey edged away from the scene and glided to his side. She whispered, "They said both of them were under arrest."

Angie used a voice that didn't invite debate. "I'm taking this one. There are things I know about her that are above your pay grade to hear." Looking at Lou, she said, "Front seat of my vehicle. We're going to have a nice, long talk."

Fen could tell by her body language that Lou was on the verge of disputing the order, until he cleared his throat. She shifted her gaze to him. He didn't know if it was his scowl or the wink that caused Lou to nod and comply.

Turning to Bailey, Fen whispered. "That's our cue to get out of here. We'll talk on the way to my apartment, then we'll talk some more after we get there."

They kept quiet until the officer at the roadblock disappeared from the rearview mirror. "You know how this goes," said Fen. "Start when you and Skyler arrived at the competition this morning. I'll interrupt with questions as needed."

Bailey waited a few seconds. She had a habit of doing this

as a way of arranging her thoughts. It reminded him of a baseball pitcher warming up before he faced a batter. He appreciated that she took her time to put things in order and not jump around. Most eighteen-year-olds would either close up tight as an oyster or babble without regard to the relevance of their words.

The facts came out like she was a veteran police officer. "This was a practice competition. There were supposed to be four teams, but the group from Sam Houston State University canceled at the last minute. A flu bug took out half their players. That left the ROTC team from SFA, A&M's team, and the Avengers. With only three teams, they had to change the format from four two-hour matches down to two three-hour matches."

"That means it was a single elimination format. How did they choose which team got the bye and didn't have a morning match?"

"They wrote the teams' names on pieces of paper and put them in a hat. The Avengers won."

"Let me guess," said Fen. "The team from A&M accused them of cheating."

A shake of Bailey's head told Fen he'd guessed wrong.

"It was the leader of the ROTC group from SFA, a student named Jada Thomas. Talk about intense. She barked orders to her players like the future of the free world depended on her leading her team to victory."

Bailey shifted in her seat to face him. "That was when things took an interesting turn. Chet Lowe stepped forward and told Jada he'd been looking forward to beating SFA's team in less time than it took them their last match. He insisted the Avengers take A&M's place in the first round. That would give them the chance to beat both teams."

"How did Jada react?"

"She puffed out her chest and told him to bring it on."

Bailey took a deep breath. "Chet Lowe turned to his players and led them in a salty song that basically told the other teams to prepare to get beat. That really set her off."

Fen visualized the scene. The former enlisted man was now the officer in charge of the Avengers. His military record showed him to have a propensity to rebel against authority. Going up against ambitious future officers, especially on his turf and playing by his rules, would be pure joy. Tales of the victory would spread and he'd be the hometown hero again.

Fen glanced to his right. "How long did it take the Avengers to win the first match?"

"All but Jada came out of the woods splattered with paint after only an hour and a half. She lasted almost two before they tracked her down and painted her from head to toe. Talk about overkill. She went straight to the guy running the tournament, some older man, and told him the Avengers should be disqualified because they violated the rules. Something about not shooting after the opponent raised a hand."

"And the response?"

"The old man puffed out his chest and said, 'Little girl, you need to grow up if you're going to play against the big boys. All's fair in love and war and you don't look like you're good at either.'"

"I bet that didn't go down well. How did Jada react?"

"That's the odd part," said Bailey with a tilt of her head. "I expected her to explode, but all she did was spin on a heel and march away. She walked right past me and Skyler. I heard her say, 'There's more than one way to win a war.'"

"Did you ask her what she meant?"

"Skyler did, but she ignored him. He kept asking her until she spun and kicked him in the belly with some sort of martial arts move. By the time he stopped throwing up his breakfast, she was long gone and so was her team."

Instead of asking further questions, Fen processed what he'd heard. Jada Thomas was likely a senior who would graduate in May. Instead of starting her career as an Army officer with a huge win to her credit, the Avengers, led by Chet Lowe, had dished out a full serving of humiliation.

Fen focused on Jada and allowed his mind to plan a series of questions to ask her. Had she looked forward to this day as a last chance to prove herself as a leader who could win a major battle? Was the humiliation enough for her to sneak back into the woods and kill Chet Lowe?

A car passed without dimming its bright lights. He squinted and focused on the white line on the right side of the road. "Have you ever seen Jada on campus?"

"I see her every morning in the cafeteria, but I've never spoken to her. She stands out like a sore thumb because she only wears something issued by the Army."

"Get to know her. Tell her your funds to attend college are limited and you heard ROTC might be a way to keep you in school."

"That's close to the truth if we don't get this case solved before the spring fairs kick off."

Fen gripped the steering wheel tighter. His mind went to the team from A&M and the two cadets that had ambushed Lou as he and Bailey watched from above. The red-haired young man believed the Avengers cheated to win, and he'd had enough of it.

"You missed your turn," said Bailey.

"Huh?"

Fen realized what she said and pulled into a convenience store on the outskirts of Nacogdoches to turn around. She continued, "I'll tell you about the guys from A&M after I order a pizza. Skyler and I didn't think to take lunch with us."

Fen loosened his grip. "That's a good idea. Call Lou and see if she can join us. If she can, order enough for three. I need to hear her account of Jada Thomas's encounter with Chet Lowe. While we're waiting, you can tell me about the Avengers match with A&M."

Chapter Fourteen

F en pulled out onto the street while Bailey scrolled for Lou's number. Before she could say more than hello, the young artist asked, "Are you on your way to jail?"

"Of course not. I have a story to write."

Fen interrupted. "How did it go with Angie?"

"Good, but only after she explained how you two conspired to keep me from getting arrested. I almost feel sorry for Skyler, but this will serve him well if he continues to pursue a job as a reporter. It's a rite of passage to have at least one arrest on your resume for interfering with an investigation. Obstructing justice is good, too."

It was Bailey's turn to interrupt. "How many do you have?"

"Six, but I'm an overachiever."

Fen rolled his eyes. "We're calling to see if you can join us for pizza at my place. We need to compare notes on suspects and I still haven't heard details on the murder."

"You'll need to call Angie for specifics. The crime scene technicians were pulling in when I left. All she told me was a single shot to the neck that did a lot of damage. The body was found near the river by a red-haired cadet from A&M."

"I know him," said Bailey. "Don't you remember? He's the guy who put the welts on your neck that day in College Station."

"I remember him and his buddy well. I have his name as Raymond Fry. Is that what you have?"

"He told me his first name was Rusty," said Bailey. "I guess that's a nickname."

"It has to be. I'm glad we compared notes. It's always good to include nicknames in a story. Makes it sound more personal."

Fen huffed. "I hope you don't mind if I interrupt your journalism lesson, but we have a murder to talk about. When can you be at my apartment?"

"Put my share of the pizza in the oven. I have to write, edit, and send out the story to all the major news agencies. I'll also need to call the editors of the local newspapers and the television station to make sure they know about the murder and my account of it."

Bailey cut in, "I have pictures if you need them. There's a good one of Chet Lowe with his face uncovered and no helmet. If it wasn't for the missing tooth, he'd look pretty good for an older man."

Fen opened his mouth to speak, but Lou was already talking. "Photos! That's perfect." She paused. "Wait. Did you take them with a camera owned by the university?"

"I used my cell phone."

"Was the university paying you to take pictures?"

"Skyler didn't say anything about money. Why?"

"Those photos may be worth something. People sell photos and videos to news agencies all the time."

Bailey took all the slack out of her posture, and sat up straight. "I also took several brief video clips."

"That's even better. Send me everything as soon as possible. I'll look at them, select what will sell, and negotiate a good price."

"Awesome!" Bailey hesitated. "How big of a cut do you want?"

"Let's keep things simple this time around. Fifty-fifty split on anything either of us earns. That includes my story of what happened today and your photos and videos."

Bailey rubbed her good hand on her jeans. "I'll send everything. We'll keep your pizza warm until you get to Fen's."

The two women ended their conversation, and Bailey went to work on her phone. The potential windfall monopolized her attention, so Fen let her finish her tasks before he asked any more about the tournament and the murder.

They arrived at the complex and Bailey continued to manipulate her phone as they walked to Fen's one-bedroom, top-floor apartment. With all the photos and videos sent and the pizzas ordered, Fen listened to Bailey for another few minutes as she rattled on about how much money she might make. She finally ran low on words, which allowed him to get her focus back on the tournament and its participants.

"Did any of the team members from SFA stick around for the afternoon match?"

Bailey shook her head. "Like I said earlier, all but Jada Thomas left while she was being humiliated. The other Avengers made fun of her, but Chet Lowe and that older man were especially vicious. Chet reminded me of a guy I knew in Houston. The last I heard, he's doing time for robbery and assault of an elderly woman."

Fen nodded that he understood. "Some people seem to be born mean. From everything I've learned about Chet Lowe, he fits that profile."

"I stayed away from him, but his son was nice enough."

Fen perked up. "His son? There wasn't another Avenger with the last name Lowe."

"Stepson," said Bailey, to clarify the father-son relationship. "His name is Hayden Lee, and he's in my intro to business class."

Fen cocked his head. "How well do you know him?"

"Today was the first time I spoke to him, and only for a few minutes. His stepdad treated him the way my stepdad treated me. Chet cussed him out in front of everyone for talking to me. Then gave me the stink-eye after he told Hayden never to talk to me or any other member of the press."

That explained it. Chet must have thought Bailey was working with Lou on another hit piece for the local papers and television station. As things turned out, the two women were now doing that very thing, but only after someone had killed him.

The revelation that Bailey already had a sliver of a relationship with a member of the Avengers seemed like a present dropped in his lap. The budding artist was turning out to be a bigger asset than he expected, but was she still willing to gather information for him?

"Could you do a favor for me?" He hoped the question wouldn't sound like manipulation.

She crossed her arms. "I've heard that tone of voice before. It usually comes before something that sounds simple but ends up costing me time I could be painting."

"This has to do with the investigation. If you don't want to be a part of it, I'll do it myself."

"Painting and helping you solve crimes is why I agreed to come here. You already tricked me into taking a full load of college classes and living in a dorm with a bunch of silly girls. What else do you want?"

"Good. I want you to get to know Hayden Lee. Find out

about his home life, his relationship with his stepfather, mom, and any siblings. Also, press him about being a member of the Avengers. Will he take over now that his stepfather's dead? What are his plans for the future? What's his major and minor? I especially want to know if Chet Lowe had any real enemies. Did anyone hate him enough to kill him?"

Fen wasn't expecting Bailey to have an immediate response, but she didn't hesitate. "Rusty Fry was mad enough to do it."

"The young man from A&M? Are you serious?"

Bailey slipped off her hiking boots and went to place them by the front door as she spoke over her shoulder. "It was just after noon when the second contest started. They divided the hundred acres into two fifty-acre plots. Strips of white rags tied to trees and bushes marked the center line. Team captains flipped a coin to see which team would go to the left and which one would go to the right. A&M won the toss and chose the woods on the right.

"The older man who gave Jada Thomas such a hard time told both teams they had fifteen minutes before they could cross the center line. He blew a whistle, and the players took off like rabbits. Fifteen minutes later, he sounded an air horn, and the match started."

"Was that any different than the way they played the first game?"

Bailey shook her head. "Exactly the same. There were two referees from each team spread out in the woods, but with a hundred acres of forest to cover, they couldn't see every time someone got hit with a paintball."

"What about cheating? Those guys from A&M said the Avengers would do anything to win."

Bailey shook her head to register disagreement. "The only person who said anything about cheating was Rusty. They knocked him out of the competition in the first half hour. He said it was Chet who nailed him from behind which was impossible to do without cheating."

"Did he say how he believed Chet cheated?"

This earned a nod from Bailey. "Rusty said his strategy was to stay camouflaged close to the northern boundary, with thick bushes on three sides. He claims he never moved because he wanted the Avengers to come to him. The only direction they could see him was if they came up from behind."

Fen put the pieces together. "That means Chet either crossed the center line before he should have or he left the property completely, came in from the north, and crossed the fence, to take out Rusty."

"That's what made Rusty so mad. He's sure Chet crawled under the fence behind him, but no one saw him do it and there's footprints all over the ground from where the Avengers practiced, not to mention the earlier match."

"Did Rusty file a protest?"

"What good would that do? He saw what happened to Jada."

"Then what?"

"He grabbed a duffel bag and went to where they parked. I didn't see him again until after the match. When Chet Lowe didn't return to celebrate their win, the Avengers knew something was wrong. A&M's team stayed around to look for him. Lou was near Rusty when he found Chet."

"Where were you when they discovered the body?"

"With Skyler and Hayden Lee, way on the southern fence line."

"Did anyone hear the shot?"

Bailey held up a single finger. "Lou and the cops who finally arrived asked everyone that same question. The only shots anyone heard all day were from air rifles."

"Now that's interesting."

"What does it mean?"

Fen raised his shoulders and let them drop. "One thing you learn when investigating crimes is to pay attention to the unexpected and unexplained. Sometimes it's more important to not hear things you should. The same thing goes for not seeing what should be there."

The sound of a text message alert put a temporary end to the conversation. Bailey retrieved her phone. "The pizza delivery guy is here. Thank goodness. I'm starving."

Instead of getting up, Fen stayed in the overstuffed chair that looked as if it had seen its share of parties. The suspect list had grown substantially with Bailey's recollection of the day. Now he had three crimes with at least as many people with cause to celebrate Chet's death rather than mourn it. He thought of the paintball bomb in the mailbox and added Pete Crane, who was both a victim and a suspect. He might not have killed Chet, but he could have arranged it with an Avenger who wanted new leadership. That left two other new suspects, Jada Thomas and Raymond, Rusty, Fry from A&M.

The next thing that had Fen stumped was the weapon that killed Chet. Angie Morse said it was a gunshot that did massive damage. What kind of pistol or rifle kills someone while making virtually no sound? A suppressor muffles the crack of a normal hypersonic bullet, but it's not like in the movies, where it makes a soft *pufft* like a paintball rifle. There should have been the crack of a rifle shot.

"Supreme or meat lovers?" hollered Bailey from the kitchen.

"One of each and a diet Coke from the refrigerator."

She brought him a plate, the soft drink, and a glass of ice. While setting the drink on the table, she asked, "Are you watching your weight for Lou or that pretty highway patrol lieutenant?"

Fen scoffed. "Angie's married, Lou's having a torrid love affair with her work, and I'm not looking." He poured the drink over ice. "What about you? Which players caught your eye today? Rusty, or the other cute Aggie that I can't remember his name? Perhaps it's Skyler, or Hayden Lee?"

Bailey took her time in answering. "It's a toss-up between tall, dark, and handsome from A&M and Hayden Lee."

Fen had the slice of supreme almost to his lips when he said, "You're growing up faster than I thought."

Bailey quickly added, "Lou's still my role model. Nothing and nobody will come before my painting."

Fen was grateful a mouth full of pizza kept him from placing a wager on her last words.

Bailey returned from the kitchen with her plate loaded with pizza and a soft drink. "What do we do until Lou arrives?"

"You can do whatever you want. I'm going to prop up my leg, ice my knee, and think."

"Where do you keep a sketch pad and pencils?"

He pointed to the bedroom. "Top dresser drawer on the right. Help yourself. What are you going to sketch?"

"People who stood out to me today. I'm going to do like you, let my mind go blank, and sketch without thinking. It might be interesting to see what I come up with."

That's something he'd do later in the investigation. Before that, he needed more facts. Some would come from Lou and others from Angie. He'd need to do his share of interviews. One included a trip to College Station to talk to Rusty. Another was arranging a meeting with Jada Thomas. He also needed to speak with Chet Lowe's widow. If the man was as big a bully as Fen heard, she might not be a grieving widow. Perhaps Angie knew Mrs. Lowe or Lou had gathered background information on her she hadn't shared with him.

He rubbed his chin as he considered all the loose threads that had sprung up like weeds in a garden. Each suspect had something against Chet Lowe. It was time to start pulling weeds and see who hollered.

Chapter Fifteen

Bailey sat on a wooden chair with one leg tucked under her in what pretended to be the apartment's dining area. In reality, it extended the kitchen by only a few feet, with two chairs and a table with a drop-leaf to save space. Her sketch book lay flat on the table, while she captured images of people at the day's contests.

Meanwhile, Fen stayed in the abused arm chair with his leg propped on a coffee table scarred by cigarette burns and scratches. The couch was in much better shape than where he sat, but less comfortable. His thoughts were a jumble of names, faces, and motives of those who would've wanted to harm Chet Lowe. He tried to corral them into some sort of order, but they kept running through the woods of Angelina County. He needed to consider them one at a time, but they kept passing each other and darting behind imaginary trees.

The ringing of his phone caused his eyes to open and scattered the suspects into the recesses of his mind. The ID on his phone showed Chuck Forsythe. Fen punched the green circle. "Bad news travels fast."

"I understand Sam's on his way. Someone else is coming to help you—Game Warden Dwayne Roebuck. People higher than Angie Morse don't want Sam on the Avenger's property until they comb every inch of the hundred acres. Dwayne grew up hunting and fishing along the Angelina. He's more likely to notice something than the sheriff's deputies."

Fen puffed out his cheeks and blew out his exasperation. "Dwayne will be better than deputies, but no one is better in the woods than Sam."

"I agree, but Sam needs to stay outside the fence."

"I understand the need not to involve civilians in processing a crime scene, but Sam could finish the job in a fraction of the time, especially when I tell him he's looking for a weapon capable of doing a lot of damage, most likely a large-bore rifle."

A sense of immediacy filled Chuck's next question. "Did you see the body?"

"All I know is what Angie told Lou. She said it was a neck shot that did tremendous damage, and no one heard the retort."

"Any ideas on that little mystery?"

"Only one. I'm almost certain the killer used an air rifle."

Chuck stayed quiet for a few seconds. "Are you serious? A pellet gun?"

Fen gave his head a nod, even though Chuck couldn't see it. "Air rifles can cost in the thousands of dollars and are sometimes used to take down big game in Africa. Some shoot a fifty-caliber round and are accurate up to a hundred and fifty yards. The bullets are subsonic, so they don't produce the loud crack you'd expect from a normal hunting rifle. Hunters can fit certain models with scopes and even sound suppressors. If someone made a clean neck shot with one of those, death would be certain and quick."

"It sounds plausible. Have you called Angie and told her your theory?"

"It came to me as we were talking. I'll let her know."

Chuck's next words tumbled out. "Another call coming in. Got to go."

Fen looked at his phone as the screen turned black. Bailey spoke from where she sat. "I never knew there was such a thing as a high-power air gun."

"They're real. Some big-bore bullets can travel at 850 feet per second and can take down a cape buffalo."

"Someone wanted to make sure Chet Lowe didn't leave the woods alive."

"Our job is to discover who. Clear your mind and keep drawing."

Fen went to the bedroom and called Sam. The conversation was predictably short, but the ranch foreman surprised him by not wanting to search the restricted area. All he said was, "Good. Cops mess up crime scenes. I'll search the perimeter and go home. If I find anything, I'll call and tell you where it is. You can tell your buddies with badges where to look."

With that much of a plan in place, Fen called Angie. She answered after only one ring. "The sheriff called off the search of everything outside a fifty-yard area from where they found the body until after dawn. What do you have?"

He told her Sam wouldn't disturb the cordoned-off area but would do a thorough search outside the fence and probably be gone before first light.

She replied with, "There's only a waxing crescent moon out tonight and the tall pines block what little light there is. He won't be able to see much without a flashlight. The sheriff posted deputies on all four corners of the fence. They're bound to see him."

"Sam rarely uses any sort of artificial light, and only uses night vision equipment when he has to. Will they post any deputies outside the fence?"

"Inside only, and mainly around the area where the body fell."

"Good. They'll never know Sam's there. I'll call you early and let you know if he found anything." He paused. "By the way, tell the search team to look for a high-power air rifle."

Angie remained quiet for several seconds. "That would explain why no one heard the shot and why Chet's neck looked as if someone shot him with a cannon. With a suppressor, it would sound like a regular paintball rifle, especially for anyone that wasn't nearby."

Fen told her the information he'd gathered from Lou and Bailey, and that he'd identified at least four people with a motive to harm Chet Lowe. He purposefully didn't include Lou Cooper, even though she crossed his mind.

Angie responded with, "You've been busy. Do you need me to follow up with any of them?"

"Let me think about it tonight, and I'll let you know tomorrow morning. Lou's coming over later, and she might have another suspect to add to the pile. For now, I've assigned Bailey to befriend Hayden Lee, Chet's stepson."

"Isn't she a bit young to play private detective?"

"Bailey's a thirty-year-old trapped in the body of a college freshman. Besides, she's only supposed to gather information on what it was like having Chet Lowe as a stepfather."

"Hmmm. I can see where a pretty young woman like Bailey could bat those baby-blues and get a man to tell her his life story. The glove covering her burns makes her look even more vulnerable, someone you don't expect to be pumping you for information."

Angie took a breath and continued, "Have you met Hayden?"

"Not yet. Why?"

"He's like his mom, quiet and mousy, nothing like his step-dad. Bailey might get some nuggets to add to our background file, but he's nowhere near the top of my list of suspects. Still, it'll be interesting to see if she comes through with information that leads us to the killer. The Avengers are so secretive. Perhaps she'll hear something of real value."

Fen leaned over and massaged his knee. "Who's at the top of your list?"

Angie didn't hesitate. "One of the Avengers. Pete Crane has the background, skill set, temperament, and motive to kill Chet. Losing an eye and being laid up in the hospital for a week would make a man like him intent on getting even. I think he found a kindred soul among the paintball team who had the will, but not the brains, to kill him." She summed up her thoughts. "My money's on Pete and an accomplice."

Fen took in and let out a deep breath. "You're right. Pete's the odds-on favorite to be the brains behind it, but he'll be a tough one to get to talk. Can you think of any way we can get leverage on him?"

Angie chuckled. "That's why they sent for you, the magician that can pull rabbits out of hats."

"I'm fresh out of bunnies. Sam took my last one and cooked it over an open fire."

This earned him a full laugh, followed by Angie saying, "You'll get the goods on Pete Crane. I have faith in you."

He promised again to call her early the next morning. Once the phone played its musical notes, he put it down and whispered, "Pete Crane may be the one." His mind played with the idea until the other suspects came calling, each wanting equal consideration.

Time lost its meaning as he turned over the conversations with Bailey and Angie in his mind. He ended his mental gymnastics with, "I need facts. You can't convict someone with motive alone."

A knock on the front door brought him off the chair. Bailey had the door open for Lou by the time he limped to the couch. "Did you and Bailey get rich by selling your story and photos?"

"Richer than we were," replied Lou.

Bailey's eyes opened wider. "How much?"

"Not everyone has gotten back to me, but you'll have enough to pay car insurance through the summer."

Bailey slapped her good hand against her thigh and cut loose with a bright smile. "I'm taking photos and film clips everywhere I go."

Lou gave her a word of caution. "What happened today is a unicorn. I know a lot of photojournalists. They're known for being overworked and underpaid."

After Lou and Bailey settled themselves on the couch, Fen cast his gaze to the reporter. "I need to hear your account of what happened at the paintball matches. Start with the first one."

It was a detailed report but offered nothing in terms of additional suspects. Fen used his fingers to count them off. "First, we have the unknown member of the Avengers under Pete Crane's direction."

Lou echoed Angie's sentiments. "That's my first choice, but good luck getting any of them to talk."

Fen kept going. "The rest aren't in any order. There's Jada Thomas, the leader of SFA's team."

Bailey broke in. "She disappeared after the Avengers annihilated the team from SFA in the first round and Leroy Clover embarrassed her."

"Could Jada have slipped back into the woods?"

Bailey turned to Lou. "I didn't look to see if she left after their match. Did you?"

She answered with a shake of her head.

Fen cast his gaze to Lou. "Could Leroy have drifted into the woods during the second match with no one noticing him?"

Lou's head shook again. "Doubtful. His sneaking-on-his-belly days ended eighty pounds ago."

Bailey nodded in agreement. "Too many chicken-fried steaks and cans of Budweiser. The only time I saw him leave the registration area was when he went behind a tree to water it."

"We'll leave him off for now," said Fen. "Next we have Rusty Fry from A&M."

"He was plenty mad," said Bailey.

"Possible," said Lou. "I know from personal experience he aims for the neck."

Fen let out a sound that communicated he'd not thought of that. "Finally, we have Hayden Lee, Chet's stepson."

Lou piped up. "I'd talk to his mother before Hayden. Rumors are Chet got rough with her regularly." She followed this with, "Didn't I hear someone promise me hot pizza when I got here?"

Bailey sprung to her feet. "Sorry. It's in the oven, just like I said."

"Did you remember to turn the oven on to keep it warm?"

"Uh..."

"That's fine if you didn't. Pop two pieces in the microwave for forty-five seconds. That should take the chill off."

"I'll bring you some salad while it's warming."

Fen spoke loud enough to overcome Bailey's rummaging in the refrigerator and operating the microwave. "Lou, you said a minute ago that you'd like to speak with Hayden's mother. Why don't you do that in a few days? You've had more experience than me in getting grieving widows to answer questions."

Lou tilted her head and tucked hair behind her ear. "Do you think she might have something to do with killing her husband?"

"Homicides are usually committed by someone the victim knows. Cops always take a close look at spouses in cases like this. If she was his punching bag, that gives her plenty of motive."

"She's a small woman," countered Lou. "I can't see her carrying a big rifle into the woods and sneaking up on him in the middle of a match."

Bailey delivered the salad. "Let Lou eat her salad while you tell her about the air rifle."

"Air rifle?" asked Lou.

"It's just a theory for now." He recounted the same thing he'd told Angie. All the while, Lou took in the information and stabbed romaine lettuce.

"That will make a perfect lead for the next article. When will they know for sure?"

"If they find it and locate the bullet tomorrow morning, they'll be ninety-nine percent sure. Forensics will be a formality."

Lou tilted her head the other way, keeping her gaze directed at him. "Bailey's assignment is to get to know Hayden Lee. Out of respect, I should wait three days before I speak to Chet's wife. Are you going to College Station to speak with Rusty Fry or stick around and try to squeeze something out of Pete Crane?"

Fen shook his head. "You and Rusty are old paintball buddies. Why don't you go talk to him tomorrow?"

Bailey joined in before Lou could respond. "I'll go with you. Tomorrow's Sunday and all I have to do is sit around the dorm until Monday. There's no guarantee Hayden will be in class, but I don't want to miss him if he shows up."

Lou scowled at both of them. "Did you two plan this?"

Fen held up his palms as a sign of innocence. "This is Bailey's idea, but I wish I'd thought of it. She's done business with the A&M paintball team, so it won't look awkward for her to show up."

Bailey nodded. "That's right, and I spent some time talking to the guys from the A&M team today. They even said they'd introduce me to a graduating senior who saw the sketch I drew. He's interested in one of himself. I can call Rusty tonight and get him to set up a meeting." She looked at Lou. "You can question Rusty while I try to land another customer."

Lou didn't stand a chance when Bailey played the work card. The reporter shifted her gaze to Fen. "I'll expect you to keep me posted on everything that happens tomorrow, and I mean everything."

Her gaze went back to Bailey. "I'm taking my laptop. I may need to bang out a story if they find the air rifle. Be sure to bring your license. You may be driving."

"Sure. I'll be right back." Bailey jumped up and scurried to the bathroom. "Too much soda," she said over her shoulder.

Lou squinted at Fen. "I still think Rusty Fry is the least likely suspect."

"Find out where he went after they eliminated him and get more details about how Chet Lowe got behind him."

Lou crossed her legs. "Everyone has something to do tomorrow but you. Sheriff Maguire, I believe you're still giving orders."

He ignored the title and the accusation. "Tomorrow morning, I'll be speaking with Sam and Angie. Answers should start flowing after daylight, then I'll paint the rest of the day. It helps me think. On Monday I'll have a chat with Jada Thomas."

"What about Pete Crane? When are you going to talk to him?"

"I'll let Angie take a pass at him first. He's ex-military and might respond to someone in uniform better than to a limping man wearing jeans."

He raised his head and sniffed. "Check on that burning smell coming from the kitchen. I bet Bailey put your pizza on for four and a half minutes, not forty-five seconds."

The smoke alarm squealed as Lou sprang to her feet.

Chapter Sixteen

Sam started talking while Fen put the phone to his ear. "I waited to call until I made it to Centerville. Do you have paper and a pen?"

The phone call came a little after 7:00 a.m., two hours after Fen's alarm saved him from completing a crazy dream involving animated paintballs. He blamed the tossing and turning on late-night pizza, sodas, and a visit from the Nacogdoches fire department. Bailey's failed attempt at reheating Lou's supper resulted in something he'd never seen—stuffed crust pizza set ablaze.

"I've been waiting to hear from you. What did you find?"

Sam had a habit of diving into a conversation when he had something important to say. "Start at the riverbank on the north side. Walk eighty-nine paces and turn right. Go another twenty-two paces. You'll have to circle two large pine trees on the way. Look down and you'll see a mound of leaves and pine needles that looks like someone covered a grave. There's a rifle in a camo carrier underneath."

Fen read back his notes. "North fence. Eighty-nine paces

from top of river bank. Turn right and walk twenty-two paces. Rifle in carrier under leaves. I got it. What else did you find?"

"Four sets of footprints, all from different boots outside the perimeter. Also, more than one of them crawled under the fence. One stayed on their belly until they got to within forty feet of a clump of bushes. There were tiny bits of paint on the leaves."

"Did you cross over the fence?"

"Under it, only once, and I stayed on the path the belly-crawler made."

Fen continued to make notes. "Were all the prints from the boots fresh?"

"All made yesterday."

"You're sure none of the deputies saw you?"

"The cop guarding the area marked off with yellow tape near the river snores."

"Will an average tracker be able to find the tracks on the outside of the fence?"

"Tell them one person moved fast along the fence line. The second made tracks along the riverbank, went to the north fence line and stayed out of sight. A third person walked down the south side of the fence and stood behind a tree for a long time."

"What about the fourth person?"

"Those prints came from inside the fence close to the river. That person ducked back under the fence and hid the rifle where I found it."

Fen clipped his pen into his shirt pocket and rubbed his free hand on his jeans. "That has to be the shooter."

Sam's voice took on a note of impatience. "Questions?"

"Are you in a hurry?"

"I'm hungry, and the donut delivery truck is leaving."

"Get a couple dozen. You earned them."

"I will."

The phone went dead, and Fen couldn't help but grin. Sam's diet usually comprised what nature provided from the land, plus leftovers from Thelma's meals. Donuts were a food group all to themselves as far as Sam was concerned. He could easily pack away a dozen and want more.

Next came the more troublesome part. Getting good casts of footprints and matching them to suspects' boots. The casts would be the job of someone else. He needed to call Angie before anyone but the young game warden trampled the land on the outside of the Avenger's fence.

When she answered, Fen asked, "How's the search going?"

Her voice had a hint of defeat in it. "Slow. I think Dwayne Roebuck is the only one here who knows how to search a grid pattern."

"Get him on the north side of the fence. Sam found the rifle and evidence that at least four people were on the other side of the fence yesterday. Grab some paper and I'll give you the details."

For the next several minutes, he relayed the location of the rifle and Sam's other discoveries. She responded with, "I'll go with him. If I understand you, there's evidence that four different people were outside the boundary of the match yesterday. Is that right?"

"Correct. You'll need to get casts of all four sets of prints and any more you might find. After that, you'll be busy matching boots with casts." He paused. "That reminds me, you'll need to see if the boots Chet was wearing match the prints taken near Pete Crane's exploding mail box and the ones found in the woods where Lou's abductor took her."

"I thought of that yesterday. Chet had on a new pair of boots, so I don't see how we can place him at Pete's." She took a long breath. "I'm not sure this will do us much good, with Chet now dead, but the boot casts from the bomb site are a match to the ones found at Lou's crime scene. That tells me whoever planted the bomb also kidnapped Lou."

Fen responded with, "Once we find the owner of those boots, we'll solve two of the three crimes."

"Agreed. What else?"

"Unless I've missed something, Chet was the belly crawler that took out Rusty Fry in the first thirty minutes of the competition. I think one set of prints on the north perimeter belongs to Rusty."

Uncertainty seeped into Angie's next words. "Are you certain?"

"No, but it fits. Rusty figured out how Chet was cheating and came back with his cell phone to film him in the act. Sam believes several people crawled under the fence near the place he found the rifle. Lou and Bailey are going to College Station today to interview Rusty."

"Have Lou call me when she starts the interview. State troopers will pick up Rusty's boots, and may detain him for further questioning. From what you've said, he could be yesterday's shooter."

Angie had her assignments and seemed eager to retrieve the rifle and complete the other items related to finding footprints and making casts. Progress would come today and a certain red-haired Aggie would lose his boots and possibly his freedom. It was time to make another phone call.

"I hear highway noise. Where are you?" asked Fen.

"Crossing over the Angelina, headed to College Station. We would've left earlier, but a certain young lady forgot to set her alarm."

"Don't be too hard on her. She's chronologically challenged."

"I heard that," said Bailey with a voice that cracked. "I

blame it on the firefighters storming in to put out a flaming pizza. It must be PTSD from the fire last Halloween that injured my hand. I subconsciously responded by not setting my alarm."

Fen shook his head. "Either that, or you forgot."

Lou cut off the conversation that was going nowhere. "What did you find out this morning?"

"Are you where you can pull over and take notes?"

"I can write what you say," said Bailey in a much clearer voice.

Lou came back on. "Unless there's something you don't want Bailey to hear, I'd rather not stop."

He poured his third cup of coffee. "Sam found the rifle case buried under leaves and pine needles. Angie and Dwayne Roebuck are on their way to retrieve it as we speak. Sam also found the footprints of four people outside the fence that surrounds the property."

Lou said, "The reception here is spotty. Send me an email that includes every detail. For now, tell me if I'm wasting my time going to College Station."

He immediately came back with, "It's essential you go. I need you to bluff Rusty Fry out of his boots." In his mind's eye, he could see Lou's face contort into a question.

"What's that supposed to mean?"

"I believe one set of footprints Sam found belongs to Rusty Fry. He disappeared during the match and I think he followed the riverbank north until he came to the north fence. Unless I'm wrong, he stayed outside the fence and spied from behind trees. When he spotted something, he crawled under to get photos."

"I still don't get it," said Lou. "Back up and give me the complete story."

"Let me spell it out. Chet Lowe cheated to win. When the

whistle blew starting his match against A&M, he took off at a full run and outpaced the other team. Once he was past them, he picked a spot and cut across the Aggies' side of the field. He ran to the fence that made a border on the north side of the property, crawled under it, and disappeared into the woods. From there he worked his way back toward the starting line, staying hidden, and looking for the other team's players as they hid. Rusty Fry was his first victim. A clump of bushes gave Rusty cover on three sides, but the fence was on his blind side. Sam found the place where multiple people crawled on their belly from the fence to within shooting distance."

Lou came back with, "How much of that story contains facts you can prove?"

"Enough to fool Rusty Fry if you play your cards right. Tell him we found where Chet Lowe hid in the woods beyond the fence and watched him. We also found where Chet crawled on his stomach under the fence and came up behind him. Then, say we found footprints along the riverbank and in the woods beyond the north fence line and see how he reacts."

After a moment of silence, Lou asked, "Are you saying that Rusty figured out how Chet ambushed him and may have done the same thing?"

"It's possible, but there's a lot of pieces that need to fit together."

Lou asked, "You seem to have this all figured out. How will he react?"

"If he has something to hide, he'll deny being on the property beyond the fence line. My best guess is he'll become animated and tell you he knew the Avengers were a bunch of cheaters. Either way, Angie will send state troopers to collect the boots Rusty wore yesterday and may detain him for formal questioning. Call her when you sit down to talk to him and stay with him until the troopers arrive."

Bailey asked, "What are we supposed to do if he freaks out?"

Fen had already weighed the possibilities and felt confident in his reply. "Sam said the footprints from the person I'm convinced belong to Rusty stayed on the north side of the fence."

"And if you're wrong?" asked Lou.

"You'll figure something out until the cavalry comes to save you. Call me when you're on the way home. I'm spending the rest of the day painting."

Fen did his best thinking when he lost himself in the kaleidoscope of colors brushed onto canvas. The influx of information needed to be sorted, examined, and double-checked. Most crimes came with a flurry of information and had obvious solutions. This case was different. It involved three crimes, all tangled together. The evidence pointed to Chet Lowe committing the first two and someone else orchestrating Chet's murder. Simple. Obvious. Perhaps a bit too easy. He needed to talk to Jada Thomas and find out if the footprints Sam found on the south side of the fence were hers. Had she gone back onto the playing field and killed Chet Lowe?

He rubbed his chin as he wondered how he could arrange a meeting with her. Then it came to him. He'd call Bev Bell, the head of the art department. After realizing it was Sunday morning, he slipped his phone back into his pocket. That call could wait until evening. His next appointment would be with a fresh canvas, paints, and an isolated boat dock on the Angelina River. Beyond the far bank, hidden by towering pines, peace officers and a forensics team would find bits of evidence that he'd have to sort. That would come tomorrow. Today, he'd paint and think.

Chapter Seventeen

F en pushed back the covers Monday morning and wished his late wife a good morning. As he made coffee, his mind wandered and soon rested on the murder case. Angie had called the day before while he was painting and informed him she and Dwayne Roebuck had located the rifle with no trouble, thanks to Sam's directions. The wisdom of adding Dwayne to the team became obvious when he discovered a number of day-old footprints outside the perimeter of the fence. Angie admitted the game warden's keen eyes noticed things that meant nothing to her. Low spots and seeps in the forest made for muddy spots where the forensic team had no problem getting excellent casts of four distinct boot prints, each from a different size boot.

Angie said that Lou and Bailey came through when they questioned Rusty Fry. He admitted returning to the north fence after Chet eliminated him from the competition. They even had him say he discovered the spot where Chet Lowe crawled under the fence and attacked from behind. He surrendered the boots he wore with no objection when the two state troopers arrived, and finished his mea culpa about crawling back into the forbidden zone. The officers detained him and began a chain of evidence with the boots.

Angie's recital of events didn't come as a surprise to him, as Lou and Bailey had called him and reported the same thing while they enjoyed another meal at the Dixie Chicken. Still, it was good to hear two versions of the same event.

More boot prints needed to be matched with the owners of the boots. Jada Thomas came to mind, but not for long. There was someone more important to talk to as first light broke through an east-facing window.

As was his daily custom, Fen spent time in a comfortable chair speaking with his deceased wife, telling her his plans for the day. He'd spend his Monday afternoon in the art department, coaching students who showed up. The studio was open on a come-and-go basis unless the students were working with a paid model. This brought to mind the conversation he had the preceding night with Beverly Bell, his supervisor for the semester.

He put his feet on the coffee table and said, "Sally, I called Bev last night because I needed someone to help me find Jada Thomas's class schedule. I'm sure you remember me telling you about her. She's the leader of SFA's paintball team. Jada has an eight o'clock class and another at ten. Bev thought my best bet was to look for her at the Student Center having a bite to eat, or in the library. I believe the footprints along the south fence belong to her. It may be tricky getting her to talk and give up her boots. Do you have suggestions on how I should approach her?"

Now and then he'd sense a nudge in some place deep within, but not on most mornings. This day didn't include a nudge. It wasn't something he'd come to expect, but he always paid attention when it happened. He'd have to wing it in guessing between the two locations. Then, he needed to locate the future army officer among the crowd of students and convince her to talk to him. The wheels could fall off his plan, but it was only Monday. If he guessed wrong, he'd try something else.

He looked at Sally's framed photograph that he always packed when he traveled. "Honey, I could use some help today with this interview. Could you pass my request up the chain of command? Thanks."

Most students, and almost all in the creative arts, despised early mornings. Based on this, Fen didn't go to the art studio before he tried to locate Jada Thomas. He chose the Student Center as the most likely place for her to frequent between classes. It was an educated guess, based on his college experience. Still early in the semester, her calendar should be free from exams, making the library an unlikely choice. Also, early Monday morning classes were brutal, especially after an eventful weekend. More than likely, she missed breakfast and would be in search of sustenance and coffee.

Bev had told him Jada's first class was in the Rusk Building, directly across the street from the Student Center. The nearest place she could score strong coffee and a quick something to eat was at the center's Starbucks. He arrived fifteen minutes early, made it through the line, and waited outside for her to pass.

It wasn't hard to identify Jada coming down the steps. She wore sweatpants, and a gray ROTC sweatshirt. Also, her shoulders-back military bearing made her stand out. She was taller than Fen expected, at around 5'10". A baseball cap covered a head of close-cropped curly hair. The baggy shirt made it difficult to tell her gender until she crossed the street and stepped up on the sidewalk.

"Excuse me," said Fen as she drew close. "I bought you a tall coffee and a scone. My name is Fen Maguire and I'm a new teacher in the Art Department. I was hoping to have a few minutes of your time."

Suspicion tilted her head and pulled her eyelids closer together. "I'm not an art student. Why would you want to talk to me?"

He hoped the peace offering would have a greater effect. All it did was raise a barrier. Time to try a more direct approach.

"I'm also a former state trooper and sheriff. I've been asked to help investigate the murder of Chet Lowe at Saturday's paintball tournament." He let the words have their effect before he added. "We can have a conversation away from all these people, or the cops will pay you a visit. They won't offer you coffee and a scone."

Her head dipped as her chest expanded and released a rush of air. "Let's find a quiet place. The woods on the other side of the Student Center are good enough."

"Lead on," said Fen, which she did after taking possession of the coffee and pastry.

After a brief walk, she stopped under a canopy of skyscraper pines. She slumped to the ground with her back to a tree. "Have a seat, Mr. Maguire. The ground is dry."

"You might have to give me a hand up," he said while keeping his gimpy leg straight and lowering himself with his left leg. "I took a bullet in my knee many years ago and it's particular how I treat it."

"Were you wounded on duty?"

He nodded, and she did the same. "I hope I don't freak out if I'm ever wounded in combat."

"From what I've heard, you'll do fine."

She shook her head. "I'm not so sure. You didn't hear me squeal when that guy nailed me with paintballs Saturday. I still don't know where he came from."

"How far into the match were you when he took you out?"

She looked away. "Not long enough. My team didn't have their finest day, either. I drove them hard last semester because it's important to have one thing that showed excellence in leadership on my resume before graduating. Now, I'll go into the army with nothing to set me apart from all the other second lieutenants."

She took a sip of coffee and continued to stare past him. He sensed Jada needed to vent following the defeat and public humiliation. But this wasn't the best time for a pep talk. He needed information, so he kept his encouragement to himself and waited.

She brought her gaze back to meet his. "It's a goal of mine to be noticed as someone special." Then came a half-smile, showing off a glimmer of ultra-white teeth. "I come from Carthage, Texas, which is about as nowhere as you can get. My family has the pedigree of a pack of stray dogs. They call me the white sheep of the family. I'm sure the irony isn't lost on you."

Fen grunted to show that he understood.

"I try hard, but I'll graduate with a 2.9 grade point average if I'm lucky. That's not even a full B and won't impress anyone. Leading my squad to victory against two of the best teams in the nation would have made people notice me. I could have left East Texas with my head high. Now I wonder if I'll be able to lead a platoon of starving troops to the mess hall."

"They cheated," said Fen.

"It doesn't matter. We lost and I'm responsible."

"Of course, it matters. Once the full story hits the newspapers, the reputation of the Avengers will tumble and fall. People always remember the cheaters, and for all the wrong reasons. People will remember you for trying to catch them in the act and making a truthful accusation. That's why you walked down the south fence during the Avenger's match with A&M. You wanted to catch them cheating."

She had the plastic lid to the coffee against her lips again when he made the accusation. The cup came down quickly. "How did you know?"

"You weren't the only player that tried to observe them crossing the fences and attacking from the rear. The story people will remember is that the Avengers couldn't win without cheating and you were the first person to publicly call them on it. You even crossed the fence and hid in a spot where you could record them in the act."

It was a trick he played on her, but it paid off. Fen needed to know if Jada was on the inside of the fence when someone shot Chet Lowe, so he came up with the second accusation. If she was guilty of bending the rules of the game, she'd deny coming back on the course. Sam had said nothing about anyone crossing the south fence.

It was also possible Sam missed something in the dark. After all, he was an incredible tracker, but not infallible.

Fen didn't like it, or himself, when she asked, "Who saw me cross over?"

"That's not important. What's important is that I stay with you until a state trooper picks up the boots you wore Saturday." He paused. "Did you kill Chet Lowe?"

Her countenance showed she understood the gravity of the conversation. Instead of showing panic, she shook her head and replied with a quick and firm, "No, Sir."

"Did you go anywhere near the river after you crossed the fence?"

"Negative. I stayed within sight of the corner where the south and west property lines converge."

Fen learned long ago that, like Sam, he wasn't infallible. More than a few good liars had proved themselves better able to fabricate stories than he was in detecting deception. Time and forensics would shine a bright light on Jada Thomas. If she was telling the truth, she'd have her shot at being an army officer. If she was lying, she'd have a lot to lose.

He called Angie Morse, who promised a state trooper would meet them and pick up Jada and her boots. Angie didn't have time to talk, so he told her to call back and he'd relay the full report.

When night fell, he recalled the time spent with Jada. He hoped she hadn't killed Chet Lowe. He'd feel sorry for her if she had, but that wouldn't stop him from filing his written report, testifying in court, and moving on to finish more paintings. By then, he might be somewhere else, working to solve another case.

Bailey was right. He did two things well, even much better than most. Landscapes was the first, and finding the person or persons responsible for a murder was the second. It sometimes took its toll on him, but truth trumped all else.

The ringing of his phone dissolved his thoughts of Jada's guilt like a packet of artificial sweetener in hot coffee. All that remained was an unpleasant aftertaste.

He answered his phone and Bailey's words came in a rush. "Hayden came to class today, and we had lunch together. Do you want to hear about it over the phone, or should I come over?"

"Come over if you think you heard something important. If not, tell me now."

"I'm on my way."

Chapter Eighteen

Fen had known Bailey long enough to read some of her moods. This one had him stumped. She didn't exactly burst through the door, but she didn't waste any time either. Her blue eyes had a double dose of sparkle and she looked like words would force their way out of her mouth if she tried to contain them.

"I found a way to get Hayden to talk to me after class this morning. Do you want to know how I did it?"

He only had time to nod before more words tumbled out. "I cut in front of him, pretended he tripped me, and fell to the ground. He apologized for the longest and insisted he make up for his carelessness." The pace of her words picked up. "We both had other classes, but cut them and went for coffee. I'm usually not nervous, but I kept tripping over my words. I don't know why."

Fen cleared his throat and said, "Describe Hayden to me."

"He's like me, not that tall and has a small frame. Don't get me wrong, he's at least five or six inches taller than me and there's not an ounce of fat on him. He has short black hair, but that's because he's in ROTC. His stepfather made him join and expected him to make a career out of the army. Hayden said he'll quit, but—"

Fen held up his hand as a stop sign. "Slow down. You're jumping from one thing to the next so fast I can't keep up. I understand Hayden takes after his mother. Lou described her as small and mousy."

Bailey bristled. "Hayden's not mousy, just shy. When I quit flapping my tongue and gave him a chance to talk, he told me all kinds of stuff."

"How long were you with him today?"

"Until a little while ago. He gave me a full tour of the campus. Did you know they have an experimental forest, an azalea garden, and several other gardens spread around campus? The forestry department is one of the best in the world. After walking all morning, he took me to the best Mexican food restaurant I've ever been to. We pigged out on chips and salsa and split a lunch special. He's frugal like me."

"Should I ask what you did after lunch?"

"We went to a park south of the campus and fell asleep under a pecan tree. Either they put something in the enchiladas or it was a food coma."

The symptoms were all there. An East Texas love bug had latched on to Bailey like a leech. This one's venom was fast-acting, but was it long-lasting? Time would tell.

The storm of words had somewhat blown themselves out, so Fen focused on the cases that needed solving. Perhaps Bailey had mined more nuggets of information than she realized.

He took up where she'd told only part of a story about Hayden's desire to quit ROTC. "When was Hayden planning on quitting ROTC?"

"He turned in his uniforms this afternoon after we woke up. I waited in his truck. He was there a long time and wasn't happy when he came out of the building. He said Jada Thomas called him a quitter, and said he'd regret not finishing what he started."

"I had a talk with Jada today." Fen shifted in his chair. "She didn't impress me as someone who'd give a young person a hard time for deciding a career in the service wasn't for them. Isn't Hayden still a freshman?"

Bailey nodded. "Jada hates him because he played for the Avengers instead of joining SFA's team. She accused him of joining ROTC to spy on her team."

He considered what he knew of the character of Chet Lowe. Jada may well be right about Hayden being in the ideal position to pass on information. Even more reason for her to hate the de facto leader of the Avengers. This was one more thing a skilled prosecuting attorney could use in a trial if something concrete came up against Jada. By itself, it meant little, but it could show she held a grudge against the Avengers and the entire Lowe family.

Fen asked, "Did Hayden say much about his stepfather?"

She shook her head. "I asked him then wished I didn't. He's a sensitive guy. His chin quivered, and I thought he might lose it. It's true he didn't like his stepfather much, but how could he not grieve?"

To further explain, she said, "I didn't like my mom's boyfriends or the creep that tried to take my daddy's place, but I didn't want someone to kill them." Her eyebrows came together. "There was that one ex-con that I might make an exception for, but he went back to prison before Mom got serious about him."

A rumble in his stomach reminded Fen he'd skipped lunch. "Do you want anything to eat or are you still stuffed from lunch?"

She puffed out her cheeks. "I doubt I'll eat tonight, and if I do, it will only be a couple of egg rolls. There's a convenience store Hayden told me is the best place to pick up late-night food if I get the munchies."

A follow-up question popped into his mind. "You said a few seconds ago that Hayden didn't like his stepfather. Do you know that for sure?"

She spoke with certainty. "He clenched his teeth the same way I do. Sometimes it's what's left unsaid that's more important than the words people use."

"What shade-tree philosopher told you that?"

"Some old guy named Fen Maguire."

He nodded and altered the conversation. "What about Hayden's mother? How does he get along with her?"

She stood and stretched. "He and his mom are tight. I think it's because Chet used both of them as doormats." She looked away, as if watching an old unpleasant memory. "Me and Mom got along until she hooked up with a long line of sleaze balls. The problem is, she's a magnet for that type of man and can't go more than a week without one guy moving out and the next creep moving in."

"Do you think Chet Lowe abused Hayden's mom?"

Bailey's words didn't exactly match her gesture. She nodded to show she thought Mary Beth Lowe was a victim, but said, "It all depends on how you define abuse. Physical? Most likely. Psychological? Heck, yeah."

"Did he say that?"

"Again, he didn't have to. It was like we could read each other's thoughts. I didn't need to tell him about my stepfathers and Mom's boyfriends."

With both hands doing finger rolls on the arms of the chair, Fen lost himself so deep in thought, he paid little attention to Bailey's next ramble. It had something to do with her and Hayden's visit to the Old Stone Fort, one of the oldest remaining structures in Texas. It sat near the center of the university and was a popular tourist destination, even though its diminutive size made it anticlimactic.

He was still rolling fingers from pinkie to index finger when Bailey invaded his personal space. "You didn't hear a word I said. Did you?"

He shook his head. "You and Hayden went to a museum."

She shook her head. "Did you hear me say I'm leaving?"

"Uh..."

"Are you listening now?" She allowed a two-second pause. "I'm going to the dorm and paint."

"Don't you mean you're going to start a sketch of Hayden?"

The door closed behind her, leaving Fen to ponder the suspects afresh. One thing Bailey's visit convinced him of was he needed to have a talk with Mary Beth Lowe. Was the widow grieving, pretending to grieve, or celebrating her newfound freedom? How much abuse did she suffer from Chet Lowe? Should he add her to the list of suspects?

The phone call to Angie Morse went through. Her groggy voice told him he'd interrupted her sleep. "Sorry to bother you."

A yawn preceded her words. "It was only a quick nap after a long day."

"I was going to give you an update of my talk with Jada Thomas, and tell you that Bailey connected with Hayden Lee." He paused. "Perhaps too good of a connection."

"I think I know what you mean by too good of a connection, but I'll let you spell it out for me."

"They spent the entire day together after their eight o'clock class."

"Uh-huh. Mutual attraction coupled with animal magnetism. Not surprising at their age. Nice-looking young men and pretty young women have a tendency to notice each other."

Another yawn. "Did you learn anything relevant to the investigation?"

"Hayden turned in his ROTC uniforms today. Otherwise, nothing we didn't already know."

"What about your talk with Jada Thomas?"

"She moved up a notch or two on my list." He gave details about Jada being inside the fence when someone struck down Chet.

No trace of fatigue remained in Angie's voice when she said, "I'm expecting forensic results from the rifle tomorrow. If we can somehow tie it to Jada, we'll have plenty for an arrest warrant. She clammed up during the trooper's interview."

"In the meantime, I'd like to join you when you talk to Mary Beth Lowe."

"Be ready tomorrow morning at seven thirty. I told her I'd be at her house at eight."

Fen ended his workday by composing and sending a long email to Angie, documenting the day's activities. He tried to sleep, but his thoughts shifted back and forth between Bailey's relationship with Hayden and an unease about Jada.

Chapter Nineteen

The interview with Mary Beth Lowe began at her home with an offer of coffee. Fen and Angie both accepted and seated themselves at the kitchen table. The home, a standard three bedroom, two bath ranch model built about thirty years prior, looked tired but serviceable. Located off a county road, nothing of significance set it apart from other homes nearby, except the logging truck and trailer parked along the south side of the home.

A plate of homemade chocolate chip cookies accompanied the dark, rich coffee. Mary Beth set a box of tissues in front of her after she completed her task of playing hostess. As previously described by Angie, the widow measured about five foot two from her house shoes to the top of her straight, brown hair. Her red-rimmed eyes gave evidence of recent crying.

Angie took care of introductions and expressed condolences. Mary Beth hung her head and nodded an acceptance of sympathy. The highway patrol lieutenant then cast her gaze Fen's way, a signal that she expected him to start the interview.

"We know this is a difficult time for you, but in order for us to discover your husband's killer, we want to confirm what you told the detective from the sheriff's office. It's not uncommon for people to remember things after a few days, or to mention things that didn't seem important."

She gave a nod of understanding and sat with hands clasped together on the table like she was about to offer a prayer. She looked small and fearful with shoulders rolled forward and a lack of eye contact. "I don't know what I can add to what I've already said, but I'll do my best to answer all your questions."

Fen spent the next few minutes asking questions that he and Angie already knew the answers to. They required simple yes and no responses. This part of the interview was designed to get her to relax, to prime the pump, so to speak, for when he shifted to open-ended questions. The pointed questions would come much later.

Once her words flowed, Fen asked, "Mrs. Lowe... do you mind if I call you Mary Beth?"

The first smile of the day accompanied her response. "I'd prefer it."

Her openness signaled it was time to move into open-ended questions. "Can you tell us about your husband's logging equipment?"

She looked in Fen's general direction. "Not much to say. He owned a pulpwood rig. When he worked, he'd go wherever they were logging, pick up a load, and take it to the mill."

"When he worked?"

She nodded. "It's feast or famine for log truck drivers. Heavy rain means mud, sometimes for a week or more. It also means skimpy paychecks. Unlike normal truck drivers, he wouldn't work on weekends."

"Were the mills closed?"

Her head wagged side to side, sending long hair swishing

back and forth. "Nothing kept him from practicing with the Avengers every Saturday. On Sundays he'd either be in the woods hunting or on Sam Rayburn, fishing."

"Tell us about the Avengers."

She didn't hesitate. "I called them his second wife." She looked down. "Of course, I didn't say anything like that to him."

It was a statement Fen would come back to. The time to press her would come later, after he'd clarified something else.

"Did all the Avengers wear the same clothing?"

A firm nod followed. "He has camo pants, shirts, and coats in different patterns to fit the seasons and terrain. The same goes for everyone in the Avengers. He'd send out an email every Wednesday telling them what to wear on Saturday. I guess it was a holdover from his days in the army that everyone dressed the same."

"Does that include boots?"

"That's where some members drew the line. Chet's feet are wide, which means special order boots." She paused and grabbed a tissue. "I keep talking like he's still alive." The conversation had to wait until her sobbing stopped.

Once she regained her composure, she added, "The particular brand he wore cost a lot more than what the others would pay. He let them choose their own brand, as long as they didn't stand out."

"Did he wear the same brand of boots all the time?"

She nodded with emphasis. "He always had a new pair and an old pair he'd wear to work. As soon as a new pair arrived, he'd tell me to send the oldest pair to the thrift store. He was particular about his boots, so the older pair usually had some wear left in them."

The words flowed, so he allowed her to keep talking.

"That last pair he told me to get rid of must have not fit

right. They were only a month old when he stopped wearing them."

"I guess Chet's loss was the thrift store's gain?"

Another nod. "Hayden took them along with a pile of other things I'd collected."

"Speaking of Hayden," said Angie in a way that telegraphed she'd come to the end of her patience with talk about clothing and boots. "How did he get along with his stepfather?"

Mary Beth moved her hands to her lap and leaned back. "Hayden did what Chet told him."

It was an answer that skirted around the question, but the ringing of her phone kept Angie from following up. She stood and excused herself. The sound of the front door closing told Fen the highway patrol lieutenant needed privacy.

He acknowledged Mary Beth's last response by saying, "I understand Hayden was a valuable member of the Avengers. Do you think he'll take a leadership role in the team?"

"No way! Like I said, Hayden did what Chet told him. Now, everything's changed."

Gone was the grief, replaced with what sounded like a mother's regret for having placed her son under the control of a demanding stepfather. If Chet ruled Hayden with an iron hand, how much more did he rule over his wife? One way to find out.

"You said a while ago the Avengers were Chet's second wife. We know he was rough on Hayden. That leads me to believe your husband was hard on you, too."

She didn't deny it. Instead, she pointed to the kitchen and living room. "Tell me what you think of my home."

Fen didn't need to look around. "I could eat off the floors and counters. Nothing's out of place. You have no family photos on the walls, only framed newspaper clippings of paintball victories. I passed a trophy case in the living room that's dedicated to the Avengers."

She nodded. "In the hall, you'll see a collage of photos showing Chet's military career. This house isn't a home, it's an army barrack. Nothing personal allowed."

"Does that mean you were a private first class?"

Mary Beth looked at him with a hard stare. "I realized too late that I was stuck in boot camp. Never made PFC... too many demerits."

"Did you tell any of the Avengers about your status?"

"They all knew, and I know where you're going with that question. The answer is I was too scared to ask for help. I didn't kill Chet, or have someone else do it for me. That's what you really came to ask, so there's your answer."

He pointed to the box of tissues. "You can put those away and stop pretending you were crying. How did you make your eyes look red?"

Another smile came, this one mixed with mischief. "A single grain of black pepper in each eye is all it took."

Fen looked into the bottom of his now empty coffee cup. He'd proved one thing: Mary Beth wasn't a grieving widow. An old saying popped into his mind. *If you keep a dog locked up and beat them every day, don't be surprised if they bite you when you let them out.*

Despite her words to the contrary, did Mary Beth find a confederate among the Avengers? Perhaps it was Pete Crane, the victim of the mailbox bomb.

The front door opened. Angie appeared in the doorway and said, "We need to go."

Fen had all he needed from Mary Beth, and Angie's crisp sentence told him she had important news. After a quick good-bye, the front door closed behind them.

As he buckled his seat belt, Angie said, "I need to get you

back to Nacogdoches. The results came in from forensics on the air rifle. They found a partial fingerprint on the stock. It belongs to Jada Thomas. Angelina County deputies are securing an arrest warrant. They'll coordinate with Nacogdoches P.D. to pick her up and transfer her back to Lufkin this morning."

Fen said nothing, which wasn't out of character considering the unexpected revelation.

Angie kept talking. "This will take care of the murder. We already know that Chet Lowe did the other crimes. You can spend the rest of the semester painting."

Fen moaned. He'd hoped that Jada hadn't thrown her future away, but the evidence told a different story. How could he have been so wrong? To come to grips with the inflow of information he needed to paint.

While crossing the bridge over the Angelina, a thought came to him concerning the mailbox bomb. He turned in his seat. "What was Pete Crane wearing when the bomb went off?"

Angie glanced his way. "You change gears fast. Already shifted from Chet's murder back to Pete?" She glanced in the rearview mirror. "If you recall, the bomb went off about ten-fifteen on a Saturday night. It's a custom among the Avengers to party after they spend the day practicing. They build a fire, cook something one of them killed or caught, and discuss the day's events."

She cut her eyes to look at him. "Why do you think that's important now?"

"What if he and some of the others were planning a coup to take over the Avengers?"

She glanced at him again. "It makes sense that Chet would want to protect what he considered his turf."

He rubbed his recently shaved chin. "Was Pete wearing his tactical gear when the bomb exploded?"

"Everything but his helmet." She maintained a steady speed. "What are you getting at?"

"I'm just trying to tie up all the loose ends. What if Chet meant the bomb as a warning and didn't intend to do such damage to Pete? Think about it. The mailbox is on a pole by the county road. Most people stand in front, pull the tab, reach in and grab the mail. They don't usually bend down as they open the door and look inside."

Angie tracked what he was saying. "Chet constructed the bomb to blow outward, not a multi-directional explosion. If you're right, the paintballs should have struck Pete in his Kevlar vest, not in his face." She kept her eyes on the road. "I still don't see why that's important now."

Highway noise took the place of conversation for the next quarter mile. Fen broke it by saying, "It occurs to me that the dynamics of the Avengers have changed. Chet is dead, Pete Crane is out of action, and Hayden Lee has no desire to take over where his stepfather left off. They're without a leader and now is the time to break their code of silence. Who is their weakest link?"

Angie pursed her lips together as she considered the question. "I'd say Hayden. From what you told me, he's ready to get on with his life without ROTC and the Avengers."

"What about Pete Crane?" asked Fen. "We have evidence that Chet planted the bomb, but who made it? It could have been any of the Avengers."

She kept her eyes on the road. "I assumed Chet made the bomb, but you may be right about him getting help."

He turned his head to face her. "You take Pete and I'll work on Hayden."

"What about a search warrant for Chet and Mary Beth's home?"

"Chet was too smart to make a bomb in his home, but a thorough search might turn up something of interest that we hadn't counted on. Instead of getting a search warrant, I'll call Mary Beth and ask her for permission to search. It will be interesting if she refuses."

"Did she say something when I left to take the call?"

"She put black pepper in her eyes to make us think she'd been crying over Chet's death."

It wasn't unusual for Fen to change subjects on a dime when multiple suspects filled his thoughts. "Lou's going to kill me if I don't call her and let her know Jada Thomas is about to be arrested."

Angie held up a hand. "Hold on a minute. When will you ask Mary Beth for permission to search her house?"

"As soon as I tell Lou about Jada and can get back to Lufkin. If she's able, I'll take Lou with me. She can interview Mary Beth while I search." He kept talking since he was on a roll. "My third phone call will be to Bailey. She can press Hayden for more information about the Avengers. He'll know if anyone else has enough leadership potential to take over the team."

The SUV sped up. "Make the phone calls brief. We're only a few miles from Nacogdoches."

Chapter Twenty

The day wasn't turning out the way Fen thought it might. Jada's partial fingerprint on the air rifle was a curveball that caught him flat-footed. How could he have been so wrong about the young woman? The desire to get alone and paint was almost overwhelming, as that's where he did his deepest thinking and answers to tough cases came to him. Perhaps tomorrow he could sneak away, but not today.

He needed to get back to Lufkin and have another talk with Mary Beth Lowe. She'd tried to deceive him about grieving over her husband. With hard evidence pointing to a sure conviction for Jada, the widow might be ready to talk without trying to deceive.

A chuckle escaped as he left Nacogdoches on his way back to Lufkin. Mary Beth wasn't the only woman playing mind games. Lou accused him of holding back information, even though he called her only minutes after he learned about the fingerprints and Jada's imminent arrest. At least she agreed to meet him at the Angelina County Jail and go with him to interview Mary Beth. The condition was she'd go after she squeezed information out of the sheriff.

His thoughts shifted to Bailey. She'd turned him down when he asked her to find out if Hayden had aspirations to take over the Avengers. In part, she had a point. Death affected people in different ways. If Hayden was super-sensitive, losing his stepfather might be more than he could handle. Or was Bailey blinded by puppy love and trying to protect him?

Fen thought back to other investigations. He'd looked into enough serious crimes to know time wasn't a friend. His thoughts skipped back to Mary Beth. Time had given her the opportunity to work out the deception of pretending to grieve by putting pepper in her eyes. Was the son following his mother's lead?

He crossed over the Angelina River on his way to the county jail to meet Lou. It occurred to him she should be in a better mood once she mined enough information to make a front-page story. As for dealing with Bailey, that battle could wait until the flames of romance subsided.

The maps program on Fen's phone led him to the county jail on the outskirts of Lufkin. A crew from the television station was packing up when he pulled into the parking lot. Quick steps brought Lou to his window. He lowered it and waited for her to speak.

"Let's get out of here before they beat us to Mary Beth's."

"Hop in." He waited until they cleared the parking lot before he asked, "Did the television crew say they were going to interview Mary Beth?"

He glanced to his right in time to see Lou's hair sway from side to side. "It may not have occurred to them to get reactions from family members."

Lou hummed a few bars of an upbeat song he couldn't

identify. It seemed safe enough, so he asked, "Did you get enough to fill a few columns?"

Her words came seasoned with satisfaction. "I parked a few seconds before the chief deputy arrived with Jada. About that time, he received a phone call from the sheriff who said he was on the lake fishing."

"You didn't get an interview with the sheriff?"

"The chief deputy wanted to wait for the television crew, but they were nowhere in sight. I told him I could film the perp-walk and make sure the television station had access to the footage if he'd give me a couple of good quotes."

"I bet you didn't tell him the station would have to pay if they wanted video for their evening broadcast."

Lou didn't seem offended by the statement. All she did was shrug her shoulders. "It's all part of the journalism game. I won't gouge them, but I'll expect a decent return for being at the right place at the right time."

He sat a little taller in the driver's seat. "Doesn't that mean you have me to thank for calling you in time for you to get the story?"

Her head turned to the left. "Don't press your luck. The chief deputy told me he received the results from the crime lab last night." Lou treated him to a hard stare. "Did you know about the fingerprint on the gun last night?"

"I called as soon as I could after Angie told me, and that wasn't until this morning."

"She needs to up her game."

He considered telling her that the results from the crime lab came to the sheriff's office first and it was up to the sheriff to disseminate the results. That was water under the bridge and they needed to move on to finding the bomb maker. Their focus needed to be on what information they could glean from Mary Beth Lowe.

With that in mind, he said, "I want to get Mary Beth's permission to look around her house and garage. While I'm doing that, see if you can keep her busy."

"Don't worry about me. If she knows anything about that sorry husband of hers kidnapping me and leaving me to freeze in the forest, I'll get it out of her."

"Ah, I should have known."

"Known what?"

"Why you were acting like a bear with a toothache and a thorn in your paw. That late-night stroll in the woods still has you upset."

She growled.

He cast a quick gaze her way. "What happens if I discover evidence that clears her husband of abducting you?"

"Didn't the boots match the prints found at the mailbox and my kidnapping?"

"Yes, but I haven't heard if they were the same boots Chet was wearing when someone killed him."

Another possibility had crossed his mind, but he didn't say anything about it because it was such a long shot. Besides, they'd arrived at Mary Beth's and Lou had her seat belt off by the time he put the truck in park.

Gone were the red eyes when Mary Beth answered the door. She greeted him with a coy smile, turned her gaze to Lou, and shifted her gaze back. With hand extended, she said, "You must be the reporter that's got everyone in the county stirred up."

Lou gripped her hand as the two women seemed to size each other up. "You're right. My name is Lou Cooper and we've just come from the county jail. There's been an arrest related to your husband's murder."

Mary Beth cut her off. "My phone's been ringing for thirty minutes." She turned her gaze from Lou and fixed it on Fen. "I understand an ROTC student at the college is the one that killed Chet."

"That's what the sheriff believes. Do you mind if we come in and discuss this recent development?"

She stood aside. "Where are my manners? Please, come in. I have a fresh pot of coffee and friends brought enough deserts to fill the fellowship hall at church."

"Yum," said Lou. "Cops and reporters have several things in common. One is we seldom turn down coffee and something sweet."

It took only a casual glance around the living room to notice Mary Beth hadn't been idle. Gone from the walls were all the framed newspaper articles extolling the exploits of the Avengers. Fen said, "I see you've done some early spring cleaning."

She turned her head and smiled. "Out with the old... I'll get something to put on the walls once I get some advice from my real estate agent. She's supposed to come over this afternoon."

Fen took his seat at the kitchen table. "Will you move as soon as possible?"

"Hayden's paid up for this semester. I have a sister in the Dallas area that recently divorced. She got the house in the settlement, so there will be plenty of room for us."

"What does Hayden think about leaving East Texas?"

She looked up from pouring a cup of coffee. The smile had left her. "There's nothing but bad memories for us here. It's time to draw a line and get a fresh start." She paused and looked past them, seemingly into the future. "At least, it will be time in June. Until then, I'll sell or throw away everything that reminds me of Chet."

Mary Beth came out of her musings and ferried a variety of deserts to the table. With the efficiency of a well-trained wait-ress, she placed plates in front of her guests and invited them to take all they desired. Fen took a wide slab of a bundt cake with lemon icing while Lou dove into a gooey homemade cinnamon roll.

In between bites, Fen got down to business. "Have the sheriff's deputies done a thorough search of your home yet?"

Mary Beth held her mug of coffee with both hands. "I wouldn't call it thorough. They did a quick run-through of our bedroom before they moved on to the garage."

"When was that?" asked Lou as she took out her phone.

"Are you going to record me?"

"I can take notes if you prefer."

"Do both if you'd like. I have nothing to hide." She took a breath. "They searched, mainly the garage and barn, after the bomb almost killed Pete Crane. I could have told them they wouldn't find anything there."

Fen asked, "Where should they have looked?"

A flash of vindictiveness showed in her eyes. "I'd start with Leroy Clover."

Fen and Lou glanced at each other. It made perfect sense that the titular leader of Avengers would make a bomb if Chet asked him. This was the break he'd been looking for, but it would take more than Mary Beth's suspicion to get a search warrant.

Fen placed his fork on his plate. "Do you have anything in the way of proof that Leroy was involved in making the bomb?"

"I'll show you after you finish your coffee and cake."

It didn't take long before the trio walked down the hall toward the bedrooms. Mary Beth opened the last door on the left. "It's a good thing you showed up this morning. I was going to throw everything in Chet's closet away today. I would have done it sooner, but there wasn't room in the trash cans and they only pick up once a week here in the country."

She moved to a closet, opened the door, and pointed. "I

can't reach it, but there's a green shoe box way in the back under other boxes."

Fen stepped into the closet, retrieved the box, and handed it to Mary Beth. She took it to the bed and dumped the contents on a patchwork quilt. Out came a collection of 5"x 8" notebooks and a cell phone.

Mary Beth explained. "Chet kept notes of everything related to the Avengers." She pointed to the phone. "That's the phone he used to communicate with the team members. Between those two, you should be able to piece together all the lousy things the Avengers did."

Lou reached for one notebook, but Fen grabbed her hand. "Sorry, Lou, it's evidence and I don't want it kicked out of court because of your fingerprints."

Her eyebrows came together in anger. "This is how I make my living. How about I put on gloves?"

He shook his head. "There's no telling what crimes the Avengers have committed over the years. Everything in the box stays where it is until someone with a badge picks it up and starts the chain of custody."

To placate her, he said, "Why don't you two go back and have another cup of coffee and something else to eat? I'll call Angie and tell her what we've found. I'm sure Mary Beth has a lot more she can tell you about the Avengers."

An exaggerated nod preceded the widow's words. "With Chet gone and Pete Crane unable to lead, the Avengers won't last. Come with me and I'll tell you some things that will make people in Angelina County wonder why they ever treated those guys like heroes."

Fen eased the bedroom door shut and called Angie. She answered with, "I'm looking through one-way glass as detectives are grilling Jada. Whatever you have to say, make it quick."

Fen explained the treasure trove he was looking at on the quilt with as few words as possible.

"Don't let anything out of your sight and make sure nobody touches it. I'll tell the sheriff to get deputies there as soon as they can." She paused. "Wait. Will we need a warrant?"

"Mary Beth is expecting officers to rid her home of anything and everything that can paint the Avengers in a terrible light. Lou Cooper is interviewing her now."

"Good work. Help is on the way."

The phone went dead. Fen wondered what other secrets Chet's closet held. He wanted to put on gloves, pull everything out, and go on a treasure hunt, but knew he shouldn't. Best to let the people with something besides a private investigator's badge handle the search. Still, it wouldn't hurt to have a good look at his clothes and footwear.

Using only his eyes, he stood in the doorway of the closet and viewed a rack of camouflage pants, shirts, jackets, and hats. Absent were slacks, any type of casual wear, and certainly not suits or sports coats. A lone pair of new-looking boots stood at attention on the floor beside a pair of camo house shoes. No tennis shoes. No dress shoes.

Instead of remaining in the bedroom as Angie had instructed him, he closed the door behind him, went back to the kitchen, and helped himself to a cinnamon roll as Mary Beth poured him a second cup of coffee. As she set the steaming mug on the table, he made an observation. "I couldn't help but notice Chet's unique taste in clothes. Everything was camo."

"You're right, but he was particular about the brands and patterns."

"And only one pair of boots and they looked brand new."

Mary Beth nodded. "You don't miss much. After they almost killed Pete Crane, he told me to get rid of his oldest pair of boots. They went to the thrift store with a stack of other things."

"Yes, I remember you said that earlier. Did you take them?"

"Hayden did. That's one thing that makes me believe Chet planted the bomb. His boots were special order and cost a ton of money. When the boots he wore in competitions started to show some wear, he'd order a new pair for competition and wear the older ones to work."

"Ah," said Fen. "Was it unusual for him to have a barely worn pair and a brand-new pair of competition boots?"

"Yes. It surprised me when the Amazon truck delivered the newest boots when the pair that was in the closet were almost new."

Lou gave him a stare that told him he was butting in on her time. With the deputies set to arrive at any moment, he finished his dessert and coffee, then moved back to stand guard over the bedroom. It wasn't long before a sergeant with the Angelina Sheriff's Department took his and Lou's statements, thanked them, and invited them to leave.

Lou wasn't happy with the swift dismissal, but it didn't surprise Fen. Most small-town cops held disdain for private detectives, and out-of-town newspaper reporters were only a step above pond scum.

To be honest, Fen needed a break from people, and Lou in particular. Something wasn't right with the case, but he didn't know what. The urge to paint came upon him like an irresistible force. Tomorrow would find him along the banks of the Angelina with brush in hand, talking to his late wife and losing himself in his work.

Chapter Twenty-One

Following an artery-clogging breakfast at an all-night diner, Fen took a to-go cup of coffee to his truck and drove to the logging trail that led to the Angelina River. Fifteen bumpy minutes later, he climbed out and set up his easel in the spot he'd pictured in his mind. It was the same location he'd been to before. The boat dock reached out in front of him as a large cypress tree stood in the shallows with its knees, part of the root system, protruding upwards through murky water.

Sunshine poked through the canopy of trees and dappled the dock with shadows. With temperatures in the low fifties and expected to top out just below seventy, he'd soon discard the light jacket. The wind took the morning off, which made for an ideal day. Once the world around him acclimated to his presence, the woods came alive with sounds from creatures reveling in the day. A distant woodpecker jackhammered for its breakfast. On the far bank, a mother raccoon brought her brood to the water's edge and partook of a riverside breakfast of something that was too far away to identify. A pair of squirrels auditioned for a cameo appearance in his painting. He didn't usually include wildlife but he thought he'd make an exception for these two as they took turns chasing each other around the trunk of the cypress. The painting took shape in his mind. The squirrels would be mostly obscured by low-hanging branches except to those who'd look for and appreciate hidden details.

As usual, he'd started his day with Sally, talking about his plan for finishing the painting and thinking about the cases. It had been a brief talk then, but now that the river stretched before him, with no other human for miles, he could speak whatever came to mind at full volume.

Fen set his painting on the easel and stood back to look at it. He'd previously established the horizon line, using a wide brush to put background colors for the sky, the distant tree line, the river, and the foreground. The oils had thoroughly dried, and the canvas bid him to focus on the foreground, including the cypress tree and the dock. He squeezed a trio of paint colors onto his palette, then blended them into the shade of the tree that would rise from the lower left corner. With vertical strokes, the cypress rose to life on the canvas.

He'd painted for so many years that his mind shifted into neutral while he mixed additional colors and applied them. The paint seemed to blend as if it had foreknowledge of the correct proportions and found its way onto the canvas, a little at a time, in various places. No need to rush.

Time had no meaning. If he were guessing, an hour, or perhaps two, passed with him painting and speaking out loud to Sally. He paused, brush in hand, listening to the silence, absorbed by the wonder of nature, giving it plenty of time to speak to him in its own way.

The distant bank caught his attention in the afternoon. His memory came alive, and he recalled the tense encounter with Chet Lowe when he'd come close to experiencing again what it was like to be shot. He tried to look through the trees to the spot

Sam discovered the case holding the fifty-caliber air rifle that killed the leader of the Avengers. His brush continued to cover the spot where he imagined someone took the shot that killed Chet Lowe.

It occurred to him he couldn't see Jada Thomas in the scene.

His focus shifted to the left. A blank spot on the canvas needed filling. He realized this was where, beyond the trees and bushes, Chet Lowe had breathed his last. With eyes closed, Fen tried to picture Jada with rifle in hand, aiming and firing the fatal shot. Again, something inside him rejected the idea.

"Sally," he whispered. "I can't see Jada shooting Chet Lowe. I know she touched the stock of the rifle, but did she take the shot?"

He heard nothing but the rustle of leaves. This took him aback because it was a windless day. A question came to him. "Why don't I go ask Jada again if she shot him?"

He realized he'd had his eyes closed. After opening them, he shook his head in disgust. The evidence seemed so clear that he'd not considered there might be another explanation for her fingerprint on the weapon.

Questions flashed in his mind. "Why was there only a partial fingerprint on the stock? Did she wipe off others and miss that one? That didn't seem right. She was self-disciplined enough to overcome a rough childhood and excel in college. Her military training taught her to pay attention to details. Would she have been careless enough to leave behind a partial fingerprint? Could someone else have killed Chet? Not likely, but not impossible."

He kept talking out loud. "Angie gave me details of what Jada said when the detectives interviewed her. She admitted to lying about staying far from the crime scene. How close did she come? She didn't have to say anything to the detectives. Why did she?"

Again, he answered his own question. "If I want to know, I need to go ask her."

His brush went into solvent as he withdrew his phone and turned it on.

"Angie, I need your help. I want to interview Jada."

"Why? There's plenty of evidence to convict her."

"Did she ever admit to killing Chet Lowe?"

"No, but you know most people lie when they're looking at a long prison sentence."

"Humor me on this one. If I'm wrong, all it will cost you is an hour out of your day. If I'm right, there's still a killer on the loose."

Angie huffed. "I may have to call in a favor from the sheriff. When do you want to talk to her?"

"Does tomorrow morning work for you?"

"No, but I'll make it work."

The call ended without the normal salutations. He cleaned his brushes and spent the remaining hour of daylight standing on the dock, staring across the river as the paint dried enough to transport. Tomorrow's interview with Jada would be his first stop in Lufkin. There was at least one more he'd need to make —perhaps two.

As he approached the Nacogdoches city limit sign, his phone rang. He assumed it was Angie getting back to him, confirming the interview with Jada. He wasn't expecting to hear Bailey's voice or the accusatory tone.

"Why did you and Lou barge into Hayden's mother's home? Everyone knows Jada Thomas killed Mr. Lowe. That's so insensitive of you. You said you'd wait until after the funeral to talk to her."

He knew he should count to ten but only made it to three.

"In case you don't remember, we're investigating a murder, a kidnapping, a bomb in a mailbox, extortion, and destruction of property. You knew that when you agreed to help. Instead of snapping at me and Lou for doing our jobs, take a good look in the mirror. Ask yourself why you're allowing a teenage crush to take over your mind."

More words tumbled out before he could stuff them down. "And while I'm at it, you didn't show up at the art studio yesterday afternoon. If you want to sell anything this spring, you need to—"

The phone went dead.

He cast a glance heavenward. "Don't say it, Sally. I know I blew it."

Chapter Twenty-Two

The next morning, Fen met Angie in the parking lot of the Angelina County Sheriff's Department. She wasn't smiling as she said, "Let's get this over with. I have a busy day."

Once inside, doors clicked open, then locked behind them. A deputy ushered them into an interview room containing a metal table bolted to the floor. They sat on chairs made of hard plastic with metal legs. Otherwise, the room had four walls, a one-way mirror, a single door, and a bare concrete floor.

"It will take a few minutes to get the prisoner. The sheriff says he wants his detectives to go at her again this morning, so don't be surprised if you only get fifteen or twenty minutes with her."

Angie crossed her arms and scowled. She didn't have to use words to communicate this was a waste of her time.

It didn't take the deputy long to retrieve Jada and point her to the lone chair on the opposite side of the table. She came in wearing a baggy prisoner's jumpsuit and hands cuffed in front of her with a belly chain wrapped around her waist which insured her hands stayed in place.

It wasn't the time or place for small talk or levity, so Fen acknowledged her presence with a simple nod. "I want to start by saying I believe there's a chance you didn't kill Chet Lowe."

Angie huffed, and he ignored her. Instead, he fixed his gaze on the prisoner. "However, you lied to me about staying away from the area where someone killed Chet Lowe."

She shook her head. "Not exactly. I told you I stayed in the area near the southwest corner when I went inside the fence. I had field glasses with me, went back under the fence and traveled in the woods until I noticed a place where someone else crawled under the fence."

"How far did you travel outside the perimeter?"

"A long way and I stayed far back from the fence."

"How far back?"

"It varied between thirty and fifty yards, depending on the thickness of the trees and vegetation."

Fen considered her response. That could explain why Sam didn't find her footprints. He walked along the fence line except where he located the trail to the hidden rifle.

"Let me make sure I understand what you're saying. You wanted to catch the Avengers cheating, so you entered their property while they were competing against the team from A&M."

"Correct."

"Then, you say you left the field of play?"

"Affirmative."

"Why?"

"No one was there. I realized the players didn't make it that deep into the property and I needed to move closer to the river if I was going to catch them."

"Then, you exited where you entered?"

"Correct. I followed the fence line north until it turned

back toward the river." She held up her hand. "But I remained away from the fence, back in the woods."

"How did you find the rifle?"

"I stepped on it."

Angie interrupted by shaking her head in disbelief. "Don't you mean you made it look like you stepped on it after you shot Chet Lowe?"

"No. I stepped on the rifle case. The skinny end came out of the leaves like a snake. It scared me half to death. My heart was beating a hundred miles an hour when I unzipped the end of the case and peeked inside. I was shaking so bad I must have touched the butt of the rifle with my finger."

Angie leaned forward. "Let me tell you what really happened. You worked your way around the outside of the property carrying the rifle in its case. We didn't know you also carried binoculars. Thanks for filling in that bit of information."

Jada sat straight; her lips pursed hard together.

"You used the binoculars to identify the spot where Chet and an Aggie went under the fence. You saw where they mashed the grass down. You crawled under the fence with the rifle in hand. You located Chet Lowe, shot him, and exited the same way. The rifle went back in its case after you wiped it down. In your haste, you left a partial fingerprint."

Jada leaned forward. "I never saw that rifle or gun case in my life before Saturday. I still don't know what kind of rifle it is."

It was Fen's turn. "Do you own any firearms?"

"Negative. The only weapons I've ever fired besides a BB gun are army-issued and paintball rifles."

Two men wearing street clothes and badges on their belts entered the room. The taller of the two addressed Angie. "Good work in getting her to admit she carried binoculars. We'll take over from here."

Angie and Fen rose. He didn't envy the day that awaited Jada. A wave of relief came over him when she looked at the short, round deputy. "You said when you arrested me I didn't have to say anything and that I had a right to consult with an attorney. You're not getting another word out of me until I talk to an attorney. There's no way you can link me to the rifle that killed Chet Lowe without forging documents."

Once in the parking lot, Angie turned to Fen. "You didn't buy that story she made up, did you?"

He shrugged. "Sometimes I try to think like a criminal, and sometimes I make believe I'm a defense attorney."

She squinted. "Which one are you right now?"

"Juries can be gullible. If I were Jada's defense attorney, I'd say my chances are fifty-fifty in getting her off. Beyond a reasonable doubt is a high threshold. She explained the fingerprint in a way that made me wonder. Also, she dared those detectives to find evidence that links her to the murder weapon. The only other thing the D.A. has is motive. I can name several others with motives just as strong or stronger."

Angie stared at him. "Juries aren't the only gullible ones."

"Could be, but if I'd killed Chet Lowe and was trying to look innocent, I wouldn't give my accusers details that made me look guilty."

"The binoculars?"

He gave his head a single nod.

Angie stared at him. "Unless you come up with something else, we've come to a point where we agree to disagree. Don't call me again unless you get hard evidence proving someone else killed Chet Lowe."

She turned and walked to her SUV, leaving Fen to consider her words. He had to admit that she might be right, but the gnawing in his gut told him otherwise.

Once in his truck, he gripped the steering wheel with both

hands. Somehow, he'd alienated three women in the last two days. Lou Cooper thought he'd not been quick enough to relay information about the case to her. Bailey was so moonstruck by first love that she'd forgotten her commitments to helping with the case and even to her artwork. Finally, Lieutenant Angie Morse didn't believe Jada Thomas' story of innocence. She told him he was on his own to gather any additional evidence.

"So be it," said Fen. "I'll pay another visit to Mary Beth Lowe. She's way too happy about being a widow."

Chapter Twenty-Three

Instead of calling ahead, Fen went to visit Mary Beth unannounced. It was a tactic he'd often employed when he was sheriff of Newman County. It didn't give people a chance to plan alibis or speeches that would throw him off his game.

Expecting to see a woman in a robe, it surprised him when she opened the door fully dressed and looking much the way she did the previous day with neat makeup and a smile pulling her lips apart. Her eyebrows lifted in a sign of pleasant surprise. "Good morning. More questions, or is my coffee so good you couldn't stay away?"

Fen matched the levity in her voice with his response. "Both. May I come in?"

"Of course." She looked past him. "Are you flying solo today?"

He followed her through the living room. "Only me. I've been at the county jail interviewing the young woman charged with your husband's murder. I thought I'd stop by."

"Did she confess?"

"People looking at murder charges rarely do." He'd

purposefully given her a vague answer while he settled in a wooden chair that matched the others at the table of identical early-American style.

She looked at the coffeepot that contained only dregs and then back at him. "We can't have a proper conversation without fresh coffee and something to go with it. You look like you could do with a little something sweet."

Was there a hidden meaning in her words, or did he read more into her comment than intended? Either way, he needed to take charge of the conversation. "Tell me, Mary Beth, do you think Chet is responsible for the bomb that almost killed Pete Crane?"

She didn't skip a beat. "I know he is."

Not only did the content of the response cause him to lean back, but the way she delivered it with absolute certainty made him wonder if she'd rehearsed it. Either way, this could be the break he'd sought. Now wasn't the time to overreact. Instead of peppering her with questions, he kept his voice calm. "It makes sense that he was. After all, Pete was challenging him for leadership of the Avengers."

She slipped a paper filter into the coffeemaker and spoke over her shoulder. "Chet was always a hard man to please. I guess it was his time in the army that caused him to adopt a way of life that followed a chain of command. He set himself up with the Avengers as the commanding general."

"What about Leroy Clover? The newspapers say he's the president of the club."

"Ha! That's rich. Leroy Clover couldn't lead a pig to a trough." The smile left her. "Make no mistake, Mr. Maguire, Chet was the top man. He and Pete got along until Chet came up with a crazy scheme to supplement our income by extorting money from other truckers. Three other Avengers joined him; they became a group within the group."

The pieces slipped into place in Fen's mind, but he wanted to confirm what she was saying. "Correct me if I'm wrong. Pete Crane wasn't one of the inner circle and he discovered what Chet and the other three were up to. He had enough integrity to want to replace Chet, but not enough to go to the police."

With the coffee scoop still in hand, Mary Beth turned to face him. "There's a lot of smarts behind that handsome face of yours. It scared Chet that Pete would take over the Avengers and kick him and the others out. That would leave General Chet Lowe without an army."

Fen played along. "I'm not the only one with smarts. Where would you look for evidence to prove Chet planted the bomb?"

Water poured into the top of the Mr. Coffee and she didn't turn around until after clicking the button on the side. "I knew Chet had done it after he told me to take his newest pair of boots to the thrift store. It was odd in that he never bought new boots until the oldest pair was really worn, but this was his best pair. He said they didn't fit right, and I didn't dare question him. Shortly after that, a new pair arrived. Those are the ones in his closet. Of course, he still had another pair which were the ones he had on when that girl from SFA killed him."

She looked away and spoke as if looking into the past. "He always said he wanted to die in combat with his boots on."

"The bombing took place on a Saturday, after practicing and a party. When did the boots he wore when he planted the bomb go to the thrift store?"

She refocused. "Not right away. I hid them in the laundry room because Chet never went in there. That qualified as housework, which was below the responsibilities of a general. Once I had a decent load of items, Hayden dropped everything off."

"What about the bomb? Did Chet have the knowledge and skill to pull that off?"

Her head tilted. "He could probably rig up something simple, but most likely he had someone help him."

"Any idea who?"

"Like I told you before, Leroy Clover comes to mind. I overheard Chet talking to Leroy about a bomb in a mailbox a few months ago. They were always coming up with some sort of booby-trap for their competitions, so I didn't think anything about it."

"Tell me more about Leroy."

The coffee pot gurgled and sputtered as she eased into a chair. "He's too old and fat to play soldier, but there's nothing wrong with his mind. He and Chet were close."

"Would you be willing to write out a statement saying what you told me?"

Her gaze tightened into a narrow, vindictive stare. "Chet can't hurt me anymore. I'll get some paper and a pen."

With coffee, a cinnamon roll, and a written statement to his credit, Fen pressed on to the next item. "Correct me if I'm wrong. Chet impresses me as a man who'd have a collection of rifles and pistols."

"You're not wrong." She rose to pour them another cup of coffee. "There's a line of gun safes in the guest bedroom." She chuckled. "No bed, but plenty of guns."

She paused and turned to look at him. "That reminds me, I'm looking to get rid of them. What's the best way to do that?"

"Let me look at them. I'm no expert, but I can usually spot something of value."

She replaced the coffee pot and said, "No time like the present."

They walked down the only hall until she pulled up short of her bedroom door. He swallowed hard.

She must have sensed his unease. "Don't worry, you'll leave with your reputation intact. I need to get the key to the padlock on the door and the combinations to the gun safes. There are burglar bars on that bedroom's windows, too."

One by one, Mary Beth worked the combinations, and he stood looking at six tall gun safes with their doors swung open. Each contained weapons of various types. He put on gloves and took his time examining the rifles, shotguns, pistols, knives, and ammunition. "Has anyone from the sheriff's department looked at these?"

"They came looking for things to make a bomb after Pete almost died, but Chet was happy to show off his collection too."

Fen filed that tidbit of information away and acted like it wasn't important by saying, "Before you try to sell any of them, I suggest you call the sheriff and have him send someone out and check serial numbers. You don't want to sell a stolen gun or one used in a crime. Once you know they're clear, contact an appraiser. I can give you a couple of names and phone numbers. Make sure they quote you a fair wholesale and retail price for each weapon. Then you can decide if you want to sell all of them together or separately. Believe me, a collection like this will bring a lot of attention."

He pulled out his phone. "Do you mind if I take a few pictures?"

"Go ahead."

He snapped photos of each gun case with its door open. What he didn't say to Mary Beth was the last gun case had an open slot for a rifle. It also contained a shelf above the rifles, brimming with ammunition. He took two photos of the shelf, one from a distance and the other a close-up.

It was time to pay Pete Crane a visit. But first, he needed one more bit of information. They spoke parting words on the front porch before he snapped his fingers as if he just remembered something.

"One more thing. Earlier we talked about Pete Crane and how you believe Chet planted the bomb. Tell me about Pete."

She shrugged. "What's to tell? He reminded me so much of Chet they could be brothers."

"Did you speak to him often?"

"Women weren't welcome at practices or tournaments. Twice a year they'd throw a big party. Venison and squirrel in the winter and fried fish in the summer. Women and children could come to those." She looked up at him. "If you're wondering if there was anything between me and Pete, the answer is no." Her gaze went to the road and she pointed west. "My goal was, and is, to get out of this county and start over. If I hadn't known Chet would hunt me down and kill me, I'd have left years ago. They cut Pete Crane from the same bolt of camouflage cloth as Chet. I was dumb enough to marry a man like that once. Never again. I can't recall ever talking to Pete, even at the twice-a-year gatherings." She paused. "Besides, Pete had a face only a mother could love, and that was before the bomb in the mailbox."

As he pulled out of the driveway onto the county road, he whispered to himself. "She's telling the truth or is one of the best liars I ever met."

Before he left Angelina County, Fen made two stops. The first was to the residence of Pete Crane. He remembered the colorful description Bailey used at the onset of the case to describe what she expected from the Avengers: Hicks from the sticks. He added bitter and crude to Pete's profile.

He considered the petite, quick-witted woman, whose home he'd visited twice in as many days. He'd have to suspend all disbelief to picture Mary Beth and Pete conspiring to kill

Chet Lowe. However, desperate times called for desperate measures.

After leaving Pete's disheveled home and the fog of profanity that hung over it, he made his way to the thrift store. In less than five minutes, he left with a pair of size twelve, EE boots.

Chapter Twenty-Four

With the cruise control set at three miles per hour below the speed limit, Fen crossed the bridge back into Nacogdoches County. He stayed in the right lane of Highway 59 and paid no attention to the cars passing him. The three stops in Angelina County produced more evidence than expected. Now he had to put everything in its proper place. He sensed all the pieces to solve the multiple crimes were on an imaginary kitchen table. He knew the best way to corral his thoughts and put things in order was to once again lose himself in the unfinished painting.

As if on automatic pilot, he pulled into a parking space near SFA's art building. He retrieved the nearly completed canvas from the back, strapped on a backpack containing brushes and paints, and made his way to the art studio. It came as a surprise to find Bailey making slashing strokes with acrylics on a painting of the woods where the murder had taken place.

His first inclination was to confront her for wasting supplies, but decided against it. Remembering how he'd abandoned technique when he realized Sally would die, he backed off. The love-struck young woman would come to him when she was ready.

Both spent the next three hours in their own worlds, even though only a few yards of distance separated them. He lost himself in the case, while Bailey's strong strokes gradually subsided. Perhaps she was getting her emotions under control. Perhaps not. "Focus on the suspects and the evidence," he whispered to himself.

Another indeterminate amount of time passed. Images came to his mind with amazing clarity. First was the red-haired member of A&M's paintball team, Rusty Fry. He had plenty of motive and was impetuous enough to commit the murder. He even admitted to coming back on to the course after Chet eliminated him from the competition.

Leroy Clover came next. An unlikely suspect because of his poor physical condition. Perhaps he wasn't as immobile as everyone thought. According to Mary Beth, he was firmly in Chet's corner with leadership of the Avengers. What if she lied or Chet had deceived her? Leroy could have seen himself as the future leader of the avengers in reality, and not just in title.

Mary Beth Lowe. Why not? She had plenty of motive, access to the air rifle used to kill her husband, and perhaps more motive than the others combined. How much abuse did she experience at the hand of her husband? More than enough for the woman to recruit someone to take the shot for her. She also had full access to Chet's boots. Fen would bet his farm they matched the prints found near Pete Crane's mailbox and the ones found in the woods where Lou Cooper was dumped after her abduction.

Finally, there was Jada Thomas, the odds-on pick by DPS Lieutenant Angie Morse, the sheriff of Angelina County, and the detectives there. The fingerprint on the murder weapon all but guaranteed her conviction.

He was well into the fourth hour of painting when an *Ah-ha!* hit him. It was as if the trees and bushes in the center of the painting disappeared and the murder became animated in front of him. A lone figure braced the high-powered rifle on the bow of a tree branch, took aim, and fired the shot. The killer took off his helmet and pulled down a camo face covering. The unsmiling face stared, turned, and disappeared into the forest.

One by one, the pieces of physical evidence moved into place.

"Fen."

It seemed like the voice came from somewhere on the other side of a wall.

"Fen!"

He shook his head and noticed Bailey's small face looking up at him. "Huh?"

"Come look at my painting and tell me what I'm doing wrong."

The image of the killer in his mind retreated to a place beyond his ability to see or even imagine. He gave his full attention to her words. "I don't need to look at it. You tried to paint when you were mad. I told you to clear your mind before painting. If you can't, do simple sketches or caricatures until your emotions are under control."

She sounded defeated. "That may never happen."

He remained silent, waiting for her to expound.

After releasing a huff of disgust, she asked, "Why are men such jerks?"

Before thinking, he said, "For the same reason women are moody." Gathering his courage, he asked, "Trouble in paradise?"

"I'm ready to go home."

"After Sally died, I ran away for two weeks, to a condo on South Padre Island."

"Did it help?"

He shook his head. "No, but I learned two important lessons. The first one was, your emotions know how to climb in the suitcase and come with you."

This brought a flicker of a smile. "Good imagery. What's the second?"

"Always wear sunscreen when taking a ten-mile walk on the beach in the heat of the day."

Her smile widened. "I'll try to remember that, but there's no beach here, and it's late January."

He rubbed a hand down his face. "Get a sketch pad and pencils. Go to the Student Center and give away caricatures and sketches. Talk to people. Get moving. It won't solve everything, but you'll have a different outlook on life by the end of the evening."

She pointed to her work-in-progress. "What should I do with this?"

He walked to her painting and answered with a disapproving shake of his head.

She continued to stare at it and answered her own question. "It's garbage. I need to throw it away."

"Good choice. Sometimes you can't fix things, but you can always start over with a clean canvas."

He took in a deep breath. "I need to ask you a very serious question. Do you still want to help me solve the crimes that brought us here?"

She took her time in responding. "I can tell by the tone of your voice that this may cost me something."

"It will, but you'll thank me for it... eventually."

Bailey looked again at the painting destined for the landfill. "Will it make me a better artist?"

He gave his head a firm nod.

Fen waited until he arrived at his apartment to call Lou. She answered with a yawn and a terse, "You interrupted a delightful daydream."

"I have enough evidence to solve everything. Come to dinner at my place. Bailey's coming and I'm calling Angie and inviting her, too."

"I'll be there."

Something told him the initial response from the highway patrol lieutenant might be cool. He underestimated her.

"Even if there's a body on your living room floor, I don't want to hear about it until tomorrow."

He pulled the phone away and gave it a quizzical look. "Sorry. I must have the wrong number. I was looking for a woman who might be interested in solving a handful of crimes, including a murder."

She huffed. "For your information, it's my anniversary, and it may be my last if my phone rings one more time."

"Sorry. I'll make this short. Send a trooper by my apartment to pick up the boots worn in the mailbox bombing and the abduction of Lou Cooper. Will you be available to arrest Chet Lowe's killer tomorrow?"

"It's not Jada Thomas?"

"No."

"Are you sure? Do you have evidence?"

Instead of giving her a direct answer, he said, "I'll set everything up for 7:00 p.m. at SFA's art studio. Dress like a student."

Chapter Twenty-Five

Fen awoke at his normal time, about half an hour before first light. He slipped into his normal routine of speaking with Sally about his plans for the day. A light breakfast would follow, and he'd be off to the university to give students advice on how to improve their paintings and answer questions they might have. A normal, rather dull day until the meeting he planned for the evening.

As things turned out, a variation in plans occurred when Beverly Bell called him as soon as he arrived on campus. She sounded like a broken fog horn and needed him to substitute teach. He faked his way through the early class by having the students review what they'd learned so far. Her eleven o'clock class had a quick exam to take. All he needed to do was proctor the test.

By mid-afternoon, he'd finished lunch and was free to put the finishing touches on his painting of the Angelina River. At six-thirty in the evening, he signed his name in the lower right-hand corner and moved it out of the way to dry.

Lou was the first to arrive. As usual, she came with a hand-held recorder. She put her phone on a tripod by an easel he'd placed at the perfect angle to capture video and audio of what would occur.

Angie Morse came in next. As instructed, she'd traded in her uniform for jeans, a cowl-neck sweater, and a puffy vest. Fen placed her in front of an easel with a clean sketch pad and pencils. After the normal salutations, she said, "I hope you know what you're doing."

He spoke a non-committal, "If this doesn't work, you can tell Chuck and Candy Forsythe I'm to blame."

She asked, "Are you positive Bailey is up to this? I'm not sure it's a good idea to put this much trust in an eighteen-year-old, let alone one who spent her youth on the wrong side of the law." She looked toward the door. "There's also the minor issue that two days ago she was ga-ga in love and just as quick, they're no longer an item."

He spoke with more confidence than he felt. "She'll do fine."

Seven o'clock came and went, as did ten minutes after the hour. Fen pretended not to worry as he thumbed through photos on his phone, looking for another landscape that spoke to him. He settled on a sunrise scene with mist shrouding Sam Rayburn Reservoir. He selected a slightly larger canvas than his previous work and set to work.

"Sorry we're late," came Bailey's voice as she led Hayden into the studio. "I had to promise an extra ten bucks to get him to pose for us."

"No problem," said Fen through a breath of relief. He faced the young man and said, "It's simple." He pointed. "Sit in that chair and try not to move."

"Is that all?"

"Here's the job description for a model: relax and pretend

you're a rock. We're going to focus on your face, so you can sit in the chair I've placed on the podium."

After Hayden settled in the chair, Fen took care of introductions. "I guess Bailey already told you who I am."

"Yeah. She said you're teaching a class this semester."

Fen nodded. "I'm not rock-star famous, but I do alright. Up until last year I was also a county sheriff."

Hayden squirmed in the chair and looked away.

Fen stepped over to Angie's easel. "Do you know Mrs. Angie Morse?"

Hayden gave his head a nod. "You're a highway patrol officer."

Angie smiled. "You must remember me from last Saturday."

Lou spoke up, "You might remember me, too. I'm Lou Cooper, the reporter."

He gave a look of recognition. "Yeah. You were at the tournament all day. You didn't make any friends with the Avengers."

Lou offered a cheesy smile. "That's all right. After they abducted me because of the stories I wrote, the Avengers aren't my favorite club."

His response came with a flat tone. "I think you did the county a favor by exposing the Avengers for what they really are."

"And what's that?"

"Cheaters and low-lifes."

With introductions complete, Fen took the lead. "Do you want to see my most recent work?"

"Sure."

He retrieved the finished painting and placed it on an easel for Hayden to inspect. "Does it look familiar?"

"It's the Avenger's land where the tournament took place. It looks different from the other side of the Angelina."

Bailey filled the air with a flurry of words as Hayden studied the painting. "I told you he was the most talented artist I ever met. Did you notice the two squirrels on the tree?"

He shook his head. "I guess I missed that."

"It's the details that mark the difference between the good and the great. Fen notices little things that people miss and includes them in his paintings. Once you see the squirrels, you'll wonder how you missed them."

Fen spoke as he walked back to his easel. "We're going to talk as we sketch you. The great thing about art is that you can do two things at the same time."

For the next minute or two, the only sound was pencils going across paper and moans of exasperation from Lou and Angie.

Fen looked up from his sketch. "Did Bailey tell you we have evidence that will clear Jada Thomas?"

Hayden's eyes opened wide. "No, she didn't." He waited a few seconds and added, "She was a pain in the neck as the leader of the ROTC team, but I'm glad they figured out it wasn't her. Do they know who shot my stepfather?"

Fen continued his sketching while maintaining a conversational tone. "It was a confusing case because there were so many people who had a grudge against him."

Angie interrupted, "More like they hated him. We recently discovered he was behind property damage, physical injuries to wood haulers, and extortion." She stilled her pencil and looked at him with her head tilted like she wanted to capture a detail. "Did you know he was doing all those things?"

After a quick look around the room, he said, "I might as well tell you because it doesn't matter now that he's dead. I knew but acted like I didn't. In case you're wondering, I didn't try to gather any evidence against him or go to the police."

Lou asked, "Why not?"

He shifted his gaze to her. "You already know why; you wrote about it in your newspaper articles. What's the old expression? Snitches get stitches?"

Lou nodded and finished the narrative for him. "The locals turned a blind eye to crimes that might bring their heroes down to size."

Hayden kept his gaze on Lou. "The cops and most people in the county aren't corrupt as much as they're protective of the Avengers. Chet was behind all those things done to the truckers."

"We know," said Fen. "Your mother told me."

"You talked to Mom?"

He kept sketching. "Of course. She and I also talked about the paintball bomb in the mailbox that almost killed Pete Crane. We knew something related it to the extortions, but we couldn't pin it on anyone."

Lou broke in, "Then came my kidnapping. Things ratcheted up another notch... at least they did from my perspective."

Hayden cast his gaze downward. "My stepfather could be a very cruel man."

"Agreed," said Angie. "The footprints at the scene of the paintball bomb are identical to the ones found in the woods where he dumped Lou: Size 12 EE. That's the size boot that Chet Lowe wore."

It was Bailey's turn to pose a question. "The last I heard the police didn't have the boots to match the prints. Wouldn't it help if they had those?"

Fen looked at Angie and nodded for her to give the answer. "We have them. They arrived at the lab this morning and they're a perfect match. Those boots were at the bombing and the abduction."

Fen immediately changed the subject as he glanced at Hayden. "I went to your home yesterday. Your mother was very cooperative in showing me the gun safes. She even opened them for me. It's quite a collection. If she sells them, she'll get a great start to a new life. She wants that life to include you."

"Mom deserves a better life for what she had to put up with."

Angie gave him a hard stare and enough of a shake of her head to cause him to squirm. "I hate to break this to you, but your mom's going to prison."

He exploded out of the chair, sending it flying off the platform. "No way. Mom had nothing to do with shooting that sorry man. She doesn't have the skill to take the shot that killed him."

"But she and your stepdad were the only ones with keys to the padlock on the bedroom and she has the combinations to the safes. We know it was Chet's own air rifle that killed him."

Fen added, "Police searched your home an hour ago. Your mother unlocked the door to the spare bedroom. They found the box of bullets that fit the .50 caliber air rifle used to kill your stepfather. Your mom said she's the only person with a key to the room, besides the one on your stepfather's key ring. The same goes for the combination to the safes. She may have given the rifle and bullets to someone else to use, but she's directly linked to the murder weapon."

Fen softened his voice. "I know this is tough to hear, but your mother told me how much she wanted a new life and how afraid she was of crossing Chet. She showed all the signs of a battered and abused woman. I bet he treated dogs better than your mom."

With fists clenched, Hayden spit out his next words,

accompanied by droplets of actual spittle. "He beat both of us, sometimes for no reason. But that wasn't the worst of it. Do any of you know what it's like to wake up every day wondering what's going to set him off next? We knew he'd find some new way to punish us, but we didn't know what or when it would happen."

"I'm sure the judge and jury will consider that when she goes to trial."

"No! It wasn't her."

Fen, Angie, Lou, and Bailey all traded glances. Fen spoke next. "I'm sorry, Hayden. Your mother conspired with someone to kill your stepfather."

"She didn't conspire with anyone. I killed him."

Angie gave Hayden a hard stare. "If you don't want to see your mother go to jail tonight, you'll have to convince me. As things stand now, I see a young man trying to cover for his mother."

"What can I do to convince you it was me and Mom had nothing to do with it?"

Fen answered for Angie. "Details and truth are what Lieutenant Morse needs." He held up his hand to slow down a flood of words. "Before you speak again, Lieutenant Morse will read you a warning."

With that formality out of the way, Angie instructed him to retrieve the chair and have a seat on the platform. Everyone but Bailey moved in front of their easels.

Hayden began his confession by looking at Angie. "Like I said, I knew Chet extorted money from truckers. He got help from Leroy Clover and two others. Leroy helped him make the paintball bomb."

"Where did they make it?" asked Angie.

"There's a shed behind his barn. It's a workshop where Leroy and Chet made all sorts of things that helped the

Avengers win their matches. You can't see it unless you walk around the barn."

Angie asked, "Did Leroy go with Chet to put it in the mailbox?"

"Chet did that on his own. At least, that's what he told me. He was proud of it until it almost killed Mr. Crane. Leroy Clover told him people never leaned over as they pulled down the metal flap."

So far, Fen had detected no evasion or deviation from what he'd already learned.

Without prompting, Hayden turned to Lou. "I'm the one who kidnapped you and left you in the woods."

Angie shook her head. "You were doing good until that admission."

With no change of expression, Hayden continued, "I misjudged the sheriff's department. They were supposed to arrest Chet for the bomb in the mailbox. If they'd done their job, he would have gone to prison, then Mom and me could have moved to someplace where he couldn't find us."

He took a ragged breath and cast his gaze to Lou. "I even wore a pair of his boots that were a size too long and way too wide. Mom told me they were to go to the thrift store, but I didn't take them until after I kidnapped you."

Fen took his turn. "Details, Hayden. Tell us about abducting Lou."

He nodded. "It started with a phone call. I changed my voice to sound like a hick. That isn't hard to do, because I grew up around here." He followed with a recital of facts so minute, there was no doubt he planned and executed the abduction.

Lou had harbored so much hatred for the person who'd kidnapped her, Fen wondered how she'd react when she faced her assailant. Instead of an explosion, she jotted notes in a small spiral book. The victim had changed back into a reporter.

"Why did you strip her down to her bra and panties?" asked Angie.

Hayden looked at the rug covering the podium. "Taking people out in the woods and leaving them to find their way out was a college prank my stepdad threatened he'd do to me. Stripping Ms. Cooper down to her underwear was something he would have done to teach her a lesson. He couldn't stand anyone threatening his Avengers. Every bit of his self-worth was in that stupid paintball team."

Hayden fell back into the chair and put his hands over his face.

Fen moved toward the podium. "Tell us how you killed Chet."

He kept his head in his hands. "You already know."

Fen lowered his voice. "We already know, but we need to hear it from you."

"The day before the tournament, while Mom was out of the house and Chet was making last-minute arrangements with Leroy Clover, I took the spare key. They didn't think I knew where they had it and the combination to the gun safes hidden." He shifted his gaze to Angie. "There's no secrets in a house that size. I took the .50 cal and its case. I only took three rounds from the box at the top of the last gun safe. Mom and Chet were used to me staying out late, so I went to the Avenger's land after dark and placed the rifle on the outside of the fence. I knew where Chet planned to go under the north fence and sneak up on people during the match. He said he'd stay in that area all day."

Fen urged him to keep talking with nods of his head.

"During the second match, I hid in the woods where I'd stashed the rifle. About halfway through I took the rifle and went back onto the course. I finally spotted him, made sure no one else was within sight, and took the shot from about a hundred yards. With the noise suppressor, it wasn't that much louder than a regulation paintball rifle."

"After you took the shot, what did you do?"

"Crawled back under the fence and hid the rifle in its case under a pile of leaves and pine needles."

"You didn't check to see if he was dead?"

"No need. It was a clean shot."

Hayden cast his gaze to Fen. "There's one more thing that will convince you I took the shot."

"What's that?"

"Jada Thomas almost caught me hiding the rifle. She would have, but she was so intent on looking through binoculars at the course she didn't see me."

Angie had one more question. "Where did the bullet enter the body?"

"The back of the neck, an inch under the helmet. It must have completely severed the spinal cord."

Angie nodded. "The results of the autopsy came out an hour ago and it's just as you described."

Lou grimaced as she raised her hand to the spot where she'd experienced the sting of paintballs.

A sniffle came from behind the easel where Bailey stood. She took fast steps to the door and was gone.

Angie moved toward Hayden while reaching into the pocket of her vest for handcuffs. He stood, turned around, and put his hands behind his back.

Chapter Twenty-Six

Steam rose from Fen's cup of coffee as he settled himself on the leather couch in Chuck and Candy Forsythe's law office. Lou Cooper sat at the other end of the couch with one leg draped over the other.

"Where's Bailey?" asked Chuck. "I thought she was going to join us this morning."

"She's in full college mode," said Fen. "Allergic to getting up early on a Saturday morning."

Candy gave a sympathetic nod. "I remember what it was like to sleep until almost noon." She cast her gaze to Fen. "I thought you and Bailey would never come back home."

"The district attorney wanted us to stick around until he was sure he milked us for all the details of the case. The wheels of justice turn exceptionally slow in Angelina County. Between the interviews with him, the depositions from Hayden's defense attorney, and Bailey and me wanting a full stock of paintings to sell, we had three weeks of long days and nights. Then the fairs and shows started."

Lou gave him a half-hearted scowl. "Your absence left me

to deal with Thelma alone. She called me several times each week asking when Bailey would come home."

Fen had his own complaints. "Thelma called me, too. I got an earful from her last night about Bailey needing to know she had a home to come to. Unless I miss my guess, she's spoiling her with a breakfast that would satisfy a crew of lumberjacks this morning."

Candy asked, "How's Bailey's broken heart?"

Fen took a sip of coffee before answering. "She spent three days sulking before coming to my apartment. She cried. I listened. Counseling isn't my strong suit."

Candy spoke next. "You gave her what she needed most, someone she trusted that wouldn't condemn her or tell her what she should do. An exceptional young woman like her will land on her feet."

He shrugged. "You might be right, but only partially. I think pulling out of the funk had more to do with her diving back into classes, producing some very good paintings, and working the fairs."

Lou changed the subject. "What's the latest on Jada Thomas?"

Chuck answered the question. "It took some doing, but people of influence made sure her arrest didn't count against her."

Lou's forehead wrinkled as she asked, "Why did it take some doing? She didn't shoot Chet Lowe."

Fen broke in with an explanation. "She showed poor judgment for going back onto the playing field after being eliminated. Jada also wasn't forthcoming with the whole truth until I confronted her with it."

Chuck added, "But she showed initiative by trying to expose the Avengers as cheaters. All things considered, those canceled each other. She's set to graduate next month and will begin her career in the Army as a second lieutenant."

Lou spoke next. "I called Mary Beth Lowe yesterday. She sold all the weapons, and everything related to Chet's log-hauling business. A contract is pending on her home. Her plan is to move in with her sister in Dallas."

Fen tilted his head. "What about a job?"

An incoming text put a temporary stop to the conversation. Fen read the message and raised his head. "That's Bailey. She escaped Thelma's clutches and needs someone to let her in."

Candy rose and left to retrieve the college student.

Chuck was the first to speak when Bailey and Candy came through the door. "Hello, future famous artist." He focused on her hand. "No glove?"

Bailey held up her scarred hand. "It's not pretty, but it works."

Fen added, "Scars are stories and make us unique." He looked at Lou. "We made a deal."

Lou raised her eyebrows. "I like stories. Tell us about the deal you two made."

"I told her that if she didn't hide her scar under a glove, I'd have a knee replacement next winter and wear shorts at the shows we work the following summer."

"Hallelujah!" shouted Candy.

"It's about time," said Chuck. "And speaking of time, I have news about Hayden."

Bailey's head jerked toward Chuck.

"The D.A. and the defense attorney worked out a plea bargain. The murder charge is being reduced to voluntary manslaughter and Hayden is looking at a seven-year sentence."

Bailey shook her head. "Seven years is a long time."

"Not as long as you think," said Fen.

Chuck took over. "Between the time he serves in county

jail and the good-behavior time he'll earn in prison, he'll be eligible for parole in a fraction of his original sentence. As long as he stays out of trouble, he'll be out on parole sometime between one and two years."

Lou asked, "What about the kidnapping charge?"

Chuck turned to Lou and smiled mischievously. "That charge disappeared as part of the plea bargain. It seems the district attorney went to SFA and endured a cold night in the woods wearing nothing but boxers when he was in a fraternity. The way I heard it, he credits the experience as something that made him tougher."

Lou released a huff of disgust but didn't pursue a claim of injustice. Instead, she had a question for Bailey. "Do you plan on visiting Hayden in jail or after he goes to prison?"

Bailey's long hair moved from side to side as she shook her head. "Believe it or not, I can excuse him for what he did to his stepfather, but not for what he did to Lou, or for lying to me."

No one asked how he'd lied to her, so they sat in silence for several seconds. Bailey caused eyebrows to raise when she said, "Besides, I've moved on."

"What does that mean?" asked Fen.

She issued a coy smile and what sounded like a boast. "I have a date tonight with Dwayne Roebuck."

Several seconds later, Fen realized his mouth was gaped open. He sputtered out, "How long have you...? When did you and the game warden...?"

Chuck, Lou, and Candy all snickered. Candy spoke first. "I'm partly responsible. I told Dwayne to call her when I heard how upset she was about Hayden's arrest."

She looked at Fen. "Dwayne told me why you stretched the truth by telling Hayden his mother was going to prison."

Fen dragged a hand down his face. "I have to admit, that part of my plan was hard to do, but I needed leverage. Hayden killed his stepfather. That much I was sure of, but paintball players and deputies had so trampled the crime scene, a decent defense attorney would have dragged out the case for a year. Also, there were so many suspects with a reason to harm Chet that I needed a confession. We arrived at the truth, but not in the way I prefer."

Bailey turned to Fen. "Don't worry. Dwayne explained it all to me."

He gave her a sideways look. "That's not the only thing I'm worried about. There's a big age difference between you and Dwayne."

"It's only a date. I've had several since losing interest in Hayden."

Fen shook his head and mumbled, "Why do I suddenly feel old and helpless?"

Bailey looked at Candy and then shifted her gaze to Chuck. "Any new murders you need help with?"

"Not yet, but..." Chuck let the last word hang in the air. "There was something going on in Kerrville, but Texas Rangers handled it."

"Kerrville," said Fen, as if speaking to himself. "Nice, peaceful town with the Guadalupe River running through it. It's quite the haven for artists, too. Did I tell you I've been asked to teach there for two weeks this summer? It's a special program for talented high school students."

Bailey pouted. "Too bad I already have a diploma."

Candy issued a mischievous smile. "That shouldn't be a problem if you want to go."

"Not a bad idea," said Fen

Bailey grinned. "It might be a nice peaceful town now, but it may not be after you get there. You seem to draw trouble wherever you go."

Thank you for reading *Murder On The Angelina*. I hope this Fen Maguire Mystery kept you turning the pages to find out whodunit! If you loved it, please consider leaving a review at your favorite retailer, Bookbub or Goodreads. Your reviews help other readers discover their next great mystery!

If you would like to get in on the fun that surrounds the writing of my books, join my mailing list. You'll be among the first to know about new releases, discounts and book recommendations. After you sign up you'll receive the first perk of being a Mystery Insider, the prequel to the Fen Maguire Mysteries!

Happy Reading!

Bruce

You may scan below to sign up or go to brucehammack.com/the-fen-maguire-mysteries-prequel.

Murder On The Guadalupe

Two murders, mirror image victims...
one trail of blood.

Fen Maguire is called in to assist a new police chief investigate a murder. The case takes a complex turn when a second body washes up and she's the mirror image of the first victim. Is this a case of mistaken identity or is a serial killer on the loose?

Scan the image below to get your copy or go to brucehammack.com/books/murder-on-the-guadalupe/.

About the Author

Drawing from his extensive background in criminal justice, Bruce Hammack writes contemporary, clean read detective and crime mysteries. He is the author of the Smiley and McBlythe Mysteries, the Fen Maguire Mysteries, and the Star of Justice series. Having lived in eighteen cities around the world, he now lives in the Texas hill country with his wife of thirty-plus years.

Follow Bruce on Amazon, Bookbub and Goodreads for the latest new release info and recommendations. Learn more at brucehammack.com.

www.ingramcontent.com/pod-product-compliance
Lightning Source LLC
Chambersburg PA
CBHW031445200726

48289CB00007BB/2301